Outside, the weather is [...]
Harlequin Presents, we'[...]
the temperature inside, too!

Don't miss the final story in Sharon Kendrick's
fabulous THE DESERT PRINCES trilogy—
The Desert King's Virgin Bride—where Sheikh Malik
seduces an innocent Englishwoman. And what
happens when a divorced couple discover their
desire for each other hasn't faded? Read
The Pregnancy Affair by Anne Mather to find out!

Our gorgeous billionaires will get your hearts racing....
Emma Darcy brings you a sizzling slice of Sydney life
with *The Billionaire's Scandalous Marriage*, when
Damien Wynter is determined that Charlotte be
his bride—*and* the mother of his child! In
Lindsay Armstrong's *The Australian's Housekeeper
Bride*, a wealthy businessman needs a wife—and he
chooses his housekeeper! In Carole Mortimer's
Wife by Contract, Mistress by Demand, brooding
billionaire Rufus uses a marriage of convenience to
bed Gabriella.

For all of you who love our Greek tycoons, you won't
be disappointed this month! In *Aristides' Convenient
Wife* by Jacqueline Baird, Leon Aristides thinks
Helen an experienced woman—until their wedding
night. Chantelle Shaw's *The Greek Boss's Bride* tells
the story of a P.A. who has a dark secret and is in
love with her handsome boss. And for those who
love some Italian passion, Susan Stephens's *In the
Venetian's Bed* brings you Luca Barbaro, a sexy and
ruthless Venetian, whom Nell just can't resist.

Bedded by... *Blackmail*

Forced to bed...then to wed?

He's got her firmly in his sights and she's got only one chance of survival—surrender to his blackmail...and him...in his bed!

Bedded by... **Blackmail**

The *big* miniseries from Harlequin Presents®.

Dare you read it?

Susan Stephens

IN THE VENETIAN'S BED

Bedded by... 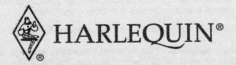 *Blackmail*
Forced to bed...then to wed?

HARLEQUIN®

TORONTO • NEW YORK • LONDON
AMSTERDAM • PARIS • SYDNEY • HAMBURG
STOCKHOLM • ATHENS • TOKYO • MILAN • MADRID
PRAGUE • WARSAW • BUDAPEST • AUCKLAND

ISBN-13: 978-0-373-12632-3
ISBN-10:   0-373-12632-8

IN THE VENETIAN'S BED

First North American Publication 2007.

www.eHarlequin.com

Printed in U.S.A.

All about the author…
Susan Stephens

SUSAN STEPHENS was a professional singer before meeting her husband on the tiny Mediterranean island of Malta. In true Harlequin Presents style they met on Monday, became engaged on Friday and were married three months later. Almost thirty years and three children later they are still in love. (Susan does not advise her children to return home one day with a similar story, as she may not take the news with the same fortitude as her own mother!)

Susan had written several nonfiction books when fate took a hand. At a charity costume ball there was an after-dinner auction. One of the lots, "Spend a Day with an Author," had been donated by Harlequin Presents® author Penny Jordan. Susan's husband bought this lot and Penny was to become not just a great friend, but a wonderful mentor who encouraged Susan to write romance.

Susan loves her family, her pets, her friends and her writing. She enjoys entertaining, travel and going to the theater. She reads, cooks and plays the piano to relax, and can occasionally be found throwing herself off mountains on a pair of skis or galloping through the countryside.

Visit Susan's website at www.susanstephens.net; she loves to hear from her readers all around the world!

CHAPTER ONE

NELL FOSTER'S shout brought the people strolling along the narrow street to an abrupt halt. The scene froze in a distorted snapshot. On the cobbled *calle* above the canal a tall, dark man was holding a limp blonde child in his arms. From the gondola swaying gracefully below him, a young mother thrust out her arms in alarm.

'What the hell do you think you're doing with my daughter?' On the pretext of helping her to disembark the gondolier had passed Molly to a stranger!

Nell's voice sounded shrill in the oppressive silence of the ancient backwater, and shock made her actions disjointed as she hurried to disembark. She stumbled on the treacherous moss-coated steps, forcing the man holding Molly to lurch out and save her. She shook him off angrily. Molly was like a rag doll in his arms, the soft breeze feathering fronds of baby hair around her face.

'Give her to me now!' People stared. Nell didn't care. She had one goal in mind, and that was Molly. While they had been travelling along the canal at a snail's pace with no means of escape Molly had fallen asleep so heavily Nell hadn't been able to wake her. It was an unnatural sleep that terrified Nell. And now this man had taken Molly from her.

'No.' The deep, faintly accented voice was brusque and un-compromising.

He was refusing? Nell looked for support, but there was something so commanding in the man's manner that, rather than attempting to help her, people were already starting to move away.

Used to wielding authority, she guessed, he was in his mid to late twenties and expensively though casually dressed. He was groomed in a way only the rich had time for—pressed trousers, crisp shirt, and with a lightweight sweater slung around his shoulders that she would have needed superglue at the very least to keep in place. He made her feel shabby, frightened and very angry.

'Stand out of my light.' Dipping his head to look her in the eyes, he rapped the words at her.

'Give my daughter back to me!' Nell met and held his gaze. She had no intention of moving one inch. What, and leave Molly in the arms of some man she didn't know?

'Don't,' he warned, stepping back when she tried to take Molly from him.

'Don't? What do you mean, don't? That's my daughter you're holding.'

Dazzling black-gold eyes equally full of determination locked with Nell's.

'You've had a shock. You're unsteady on your feet. If you fall into the canal, who will rescue you?' He glanced at Molly lying insensible in his arms, turning the question into a rebuke.

A few locks of inky black hair had fallen into his eyes as he spoke—the only part of him that had resisted perfection. Nell resented absorbing that much about him. 'We need help. Can't you see?' She fumbled for her phone while the sun beat down on her shoulders, making it impossible to breathe. The man holding Molly seemed to exist in a bubble of air-conditioning.

'You're overwrought,' he said coldly.

Overwrought? 'Are you surprised?' She watched with mounting anger as he pulled out a phone and flipped it open. It seemed like another tactic to avoid giving Molly back to her. 'Who are you calling?'

He paused with the mobile halfway to his ear. 'An ambulance.'

'An ambulance?' Nell's mouth dried. Briefly, her mind refused to accept the possibility of an ambulance coming down the canal. But she knew there had to be some means by which emergency cases could be transported to hospital in Venice.

Emergency cases? Molly was only eighteen months old! She'd never had a day's illness in her life.

Nell stared at the man more intently. 'Who are you?' she demanded.

He pressed his lips together and shook his head as he listened to the voice at the other end of the phone line.

Nell gazed at Molly lying in his arms. She was almost frightened to touch her own daughter. Molly looked so frail, as if all the life had leached out of her.

The man started speaking rapidly in Italian. Nell had found the language an interesting challenge earlier, but now it was just a hostile barrier she couldn't cross. Her heart jerked as his phone snapped shut. Why didn't he say something? Couldn't he see she was desperate for information? But all his attention was focused on Molly. His brow was furrowed and she could see he was worried. It endorsed her own fears. Why wouldn't Molly wake up? No one slept like this unless there was something seriously wrong.

When he moved she followed him into the shade. 'Will the ambulance be long?'

'No.'

'So, do you know what's wrong?' She ran a hand through

her hair. Why should she assume he knew anything? But she was desperate. She didn't know what was happening, she didn't know him—she didn't know anything. 'Who are you?'

Panic was rising inside her chest. She fought it back, forcing herself to concentrate as he started to say something. She couldn't afford to go to pieces.

'I'm a doctor—a medical practitioner.' He held her gaze fast in a blaze of self-assurance.

If that was meant to reassure her, it had the opposite effect. All the panic and fear drained out of her to be replaced by dread. She had been brought up to trust and respect the medical profession, and she'd had no reason to change that opinion until a catastrophic event had pulled the wool from her eyes.

'My name is Dottore Luca Barbaro.'

The man had moved on smoothly to introductions, Nell realised. It was as if she were watching a horror film in slow motion, a film that had no connection with her life. 'Dr Barbaro,' she repeated distractedly.

'That's right.'

He sounded as though he expected her to fall on her knees and give thanks.

'Well, now that you've made your call, *Dr* Barbaro, you can give my daughter back to me!'

'Don't you trust me?' His brow furrowed.

'*Trust* you? Why should I trust you?'

'You're in shock,' he said, sounding irritable. 'It's better if I hold her.'

Better? What could be better than for a child to be held by its own mother? 'I'm not in shock. Give her to me.' The urge to rip Molly from his arms was growing every moment, but she couldn't risk manhandling Molly, not when there was something so obviously wrong.

Nell's mind darted about, trying to land on a sensible course of action, but nothing made sense—especially this man appearing out of the blue to take charge of their lives. 'Have you been following us?' she said suspiciously.

'Following you?' His eyes mirrored his impatience.

'Oh, so you just happened along. And you tell me you're a doctor. Quite convenient, don't you think?'

'Why should I lie to you? I *am* a doctor. I live just over there.' He jutted out his chin to indicate some building.

She didn't look. She had no intention of staring at a place she had no wish to see. 'And you were standing by your window when our gondola floated past?'

'Your gondolier rang to warn me you were on your way.'

That seemed so incongruous, it had to be impossible. Then Nell remembered the gondolier *had* made a call. It was so easy to be seduced by ravishingly beautiful and apparently unchanged Venice, and forget how easily the modern world co-existed with the old.

'Luck was smiling on you,' he remarked.

'Luck?' It was Nell's turn to snap.

'Lucky for you your gondolier knew me and where I live. Marco only had to ring to check that I was in, and then he brought you straight here.'

'He brought us here intentionally?'

'He was trying to help you.'

A fact that seemed lost on the child's mother, Luca thought. He eased his neck. His head was thumping. Sleep deprivation had finally claimed him. This was supposed to be his day off, but when the call came suggesting a worrying case, his time on duty had slipped into its third day. That didn't matter. The patient came first. The patient always came first.

'The gondolier brought you here as quickly as he could.'

His tolerance levels, thin at the best of times when dealing with civilians, were at an all-time low. While one part of his brain knew it was routine for the mother to be concerned and emotional, the other, more forceful side resented her interference. The result? He was spitting out words to drive his message home. And the message was: Leave me to deal with this. I don't need to be here, I don't want your thanks, just don't expect me to be your emotional support when I have a job to do.

But there was no nurse here to take the woman away. Grinding his jaw, Luca attempted to calm her down. Human decency demanded that much of him. 'Marco could see you needed a doctor, so he brought you to me. Didn't you tell him you needed help?'

'I didn't think he understood.'

'He didn't. Lucky for you he used his initiative.'

Oh, forget human decency. He was just too damn tired, and the child needed all his attention. Besides, there was something else nagging at him—something that meant he had to be harsh. Feelings, thoughts, all of them inappropriate, were swimming round his head, pulling his eyes to her body when they should be on the patient.

He didn't need this. A particularly harrowing shift had left him tired and susceptible—how else could he explain the way he was reacting to her?

Luca turned back to the patient in his arms before he had chance to lock eyes with her mother.

'What are you doing now?' Nell tensed as he inspected Molly's fingernails.

'You're going to have to put your mistrust of doctors on hold while I check my patient.'

His *patient?* Her baby. Her life. Nell gritted her teeth. And as for putting her mistrust on hold...! Didn't this just underline everything she felt about doctors? Didn't this man's detached manner justify all the ugly emotion welling inside her now—emotion so close to hatred it was impossible to tell the difference?

'So, what exactly are you checking, *Doctor*?'

'Oxygen levels.'

'And you can do that just from staring at my daughter's hand?'

'I can see if the nails are pink and healthy, or if they are tinged with blue.'

'Blue? Let me see!' Fear welled in Nell's throat. She had no medical training to draw on. She didn't know if Molly's nails were pink enough. What kind of mother didn't know the colour of her own daughter's nails? Why hadn't she noticed the colour of Molly's nails when she was well so she had something to compare them with now?

'You can't be expected to know everything.'

And now he could read minds? She doubted he was trying to placate her. In any case, she didn't want his understanding: she wanted facts. 'How can I help if you don't tell me what's going on?'

'You can't help,' he said flatly.

'So a mother's care is worth nothing?'

'I didn't say that,' he said wearily.

'Then give her to me.' Nell's tone sharpened.

He levelled a gaze on her face. 'If you want me to assess her medical condition you'll leave her where she is.'

'You're a doctor and you don't know what's wrong with her yet?'

'I can't be certain—'

'But you must have some idea.'

'Stop pressing me for answers. You should try to relax—'

'*Relax?*'

'All right, then, how about trusting me?'

'Why should I trust you? I don't know you. You could be anyone!'

'Look, just stay calm, or move away. You're disturbing my patient.'

Nell held her ground. 'Your patient is my daughter! If you're not capable of helping Molly then I'm going to find someone who is.'

'Where?'

He fired the word back at her. She flinched and fell silent.

'If you just stay calm everything will be all right,' he told her.

The man's assurance infuriated her. He had intoned the platitude in the way Nell was beginning to think must be dished out along with the accreditation MD. 'And maybe I could stay calm if I thought you had any idea what was wrong with my daughter.'

'I can't be sure of anything yet.'

'Or you don't know.' She had been too trusting once before, and that had ended in tragedy. She wasn't going to make that same mistake again. Not with Molly.

When her husband, Jake, had been killed in a car accident, Nell hadn't known that Molly's father might have survived had the junior doctor mistakenly sent to tend him at the roadside been properly trained. Later, in Casualty, she had believed the medics had been trying to save Jake's life, not covering for their colleague's mistake. When they had finally admitted Jake was dead it had come as a complete shock to her. There had been no warning, no preparation at all.

It had been a life-changing event that had led to Nell starting a campaign to help others in a similar plight. That campaign was now a charitable trust with volunteers countrywide in the United Kingdom. People who could liaise with the medical staff within a hospital and give whatever support was required to a patient's relative or friend.

This Luca Barbaro seemed too glamorous, too young, to be an experienced doctor. Very like the young medic who had tended Jake. Nell's heart lurched.

'Can you call the hospital? Tell them I want someone there as soon as we arrive—a paediatric consultant, someone experienced. The best!'

'I'll see what I can do.' His voice was bordering on sarcastic.

'Not good enough,' she said sharply.

His answer was to lock his fingers under Molly, as if she was about to do something stupid like snatch Molly from him. Or was it just to drive home the message that he was in charge?

He leaned over the canal at a perilous angle to peer down it—with Molly in his arms. Nell's hands balled into fists. Molly's tiny frame suspended over murky water! Her head was banging with tension by the time he straightened up to stare at her in silence. Did he expect her to start a conversation—about the weather, maybe?

'You should tell me your name.'

Her eyes had to be registering astonishment, Nell knew. This wasn't some social gathering where it was mandatory to engage in small talk. She didn't want to chat with him. She didn't want to get to know him. She didn't want to tell him her name. 'Perhaps you should tell me what you know about Molly's condition.'

Nell's brave front dissolved as Luca Barbaro held her gaze. There was something in his eyes that made her heart lurch with dread. How bad was it? Why didn't he say something to reassure her? Was it because there was nothing *to* say?

'You'll have to tell me your name sooner or later.'

A doctor possessed any number of strategies for winkling out facts from distressed relatives, as she knew only too well, but giving her name as Molly's next of kin was mandatory. 'My name is Nell Foster,' she offered stiffly.

'And the child's name?'

'My daughter's name is Molly.' Nell had drawn herself up, thinking she was ready for him. But the moment she spoke Molly's name her self-assurance disappeared. Molly was the one fixed point in her life, a point around which everything else in her world revolved. Everything she did, thought, or planned was for Molly. As tears welled behind her eyes, she only managed to hold herself together by staring fixedly at her baby.

'Molly Foster,' he murmured. 'Very nice.'

The tender note in his voice took Nell by surprise. Her mouth tightened. She didn't want his smiles or reassurance. She wanted the answer to one simple question: why had Molly been taken ill?

'So, Molly…'

She refocused, hearing his crooning tone. No one spoke to Molly like that except for her.

'Is this your first visit to Venice, Molly?' he continued, oblivious to the distress he was causing.

'Yes, it is,' Nell answered for her daughter stiffly. The rational side of her brain told her that he was watching for signs as he spoke to Molly, clues that might help him to arrive at a diagnosis. The emotional side of her brain didn't trust him to get it right. She didn't trust *any* doctor.

And then he glanced up as if sensing her appraisal. She must have swayed, because the next thing she knew his free hand was under her arm and he was steadying her, and the sensation was shooting up her arm like…

She pulled free with surprise. It was hard to believe his touch had affected her so acutely. How could she respond to a man at a time like this? It disgusted her. It was as if her body was tuned to a different frequency from her mind and she had no control over it. As he moved she was forced to move with him to stay close to Molly, but she took care to keep her distance from the man holding her.

'That's better,' he said infuriatingly, as if Nell had moved into the very spot he would have chosen for her. 'You should stand well back from the canal. You've had a shock and we don't want any accidents.'

We? She guessed that was the type of nursery-speak he used in the hospital. It was exactly the type of thing she had made it her crusade to abolish.

'Molly needs you to be strong. She's very poorly. You do understand that?'

Nell's stomach clenched with fear. 'Of course I understand.' But she didn't understand any of it. How could Molly be so sick? She wanted him to say it was a mistake. She wanted Molly to wake up.

'Take some deep breaths, Nell. It will help.'

Nell's face was hostile as she stared up. She wasn't the one in need of help here! And she felt Barbaro's use of her first name as another outrage. While she had been waiting in the hospital for Jake she had noticed that all the patients were addressed by their first names. She had also noticed that no one called out, 'Hey, John,' to Jake's consultant, but had addressed him respectfully as Mr Delaware. She had resented it then, she resented it now. But she had to let it go. Resentment didn't help Molly. She recommended breathing exercises to her volunteers to use in moments of stress, and tried them now. Gradually the muscles in her chest began to release—but he was leaning over the canal again.

'Must you do that?'

Rocking back on his heels, Luca Barbaro stared down at her. 'I'm looking for the ambulance.'

Did that give him the excuse to expose Molly to risk?

'Well, don't do it while you've got my daughter in your arms. Or give her back to me.'

'No.'

She couldn't risk a tussle that might land them all in the water. She had to content herself with stroking Molly's brow, which had grown warm and clammy. Her chest was working like a miniature bellows, while her cheeks were unnaturally pink. 'Does she have a fever?'

'I'll know more when we reach the hospital and I can run some tests.'

'So, in fact, you know damn all?' Hot and cold waves of terror were washing over her. She knew she shouldn't shout, or lose her cool, but some atavistic instinct was shouting at her to take Molly and run...find help. But where would she run to? She was lost in the maze of backwaters that made up the hidden face of Venice. This *calle* was a long way from the regular tourist trail with its friendly vendors and signposts to the main attractions. Her knowledge of Italian was minimal, and she would lose valuable time trying to find her way back to the Grand Canal...time Molly might not have.

Nell's heart pounded as her mind filled with a deep and unreasonable hatred of Venice. Everything that had seemed so beautiful, so charming when they had first arrived had turned an ugly face on them. She glanced around, wondering if the dilapidation harboured the blight that had infected Molly—or the water, perhaps? The unusual silence of the traffic-free centre, which so recently she had enjoyed, now represented isolation; the lack of signposts seemed now to be a ploy to confuse the unwary tourist. And worst of all, Venice had welded her to this stranger, a man who said he was a doctor. And even if he was a doctor, for all she knew Luca Barbaro was a podiatric surgeon, happier sawing off bunions than treating children! But she was stuck with him. She couldn't risk setting out on her own with Molly and getting lost.

It was her fault. She shouldn't have brought Molly so far from home for a holiday. But then Jake's accident had happened at the end of their road—on familiar territory... The policewoman sent to break the news and comfort her afterwards had said that was where so many accidents happened, when people let their concentration slip after a long journey. And of course, it hadn't helped that Jake had had a secret life to distract him. It was hardly surprising he'd gone off the road.

The accident had happened on a Friday night, when Casualty was like a war zone. She had been locked inside her thoughts, fearing the worst, hoping for the best, when the scream came. It had been a woman's scream, a scream that connected with Nell on so deep a level she had known her whole life was somehow wrapped up in it. When they finally allowed her into Jake's room, no one had warned her that he wasn't alone. The last thing she had been expecting to find was a young woman with a tiny baby in her arms, weeping by her dead husband's bed.

CHAPTER TWO

'WHAT are you doing?' Nell refocused as Barbaro fished out his phone again.

'Calling the ambulance service.'

Was it possible to edit the information he gave out any more? 'Why?' she pressed insistently.

'To make sure there isn't a hold-up. My patient needs proper care, which I can't give here.' He glanced around then held Nell's stare as if daring her to argue.

Nell had to force herself not to shout. He was talking about Molly so impassively, as if he were a puppet master working them from the remotest reaches of his ivory tower. She shuddered involuntarily. The past, horrific as that had been, was nothing compared to this.

'Tell me everything you can remember about the day.'

To keep her busy and distracted, Nell suspected as dark eyes probed her thoughts. She wanted time to collect herself, to examine her own actions. If she had done something wrong to bring Molly to this point, then she wanted to be the first to know. 'Molly was quite well when we woke up this morning.' A faint smile touched Nell's lips as she remembered the light-hearted start to their day.

'Cast your mind back to the moment when you first noticed signs of deterioration.'

'Deterioration?' The ugly word wiped out anything good about a day earmarked for pleasure that had tilted on its axis to reveal a face as sinister and outlandish as any of the painted masks she had seen in Venice.

'Can't you remember when she first slipped into this state?'

'If you mean, do I remember when Molly fell so deeply asleep I couldn't wake her?' The way he was speaking…so remote, so detached. She couldn't bear it. She *wouldn't* bear it.

'That's right,' he went on. 'Tell me when the patient—'

'My daughter's name is Molly.' She would not have him discussing Molly as though she were some test case in a textbook.

'When Molly first became sleepy.'

Nell shook her head as she thought it through out loud. 'Why did I wait for a problem to become a crisis?'

'Because you thought she was only sleeping.'

She hadn't been speaking to Luca Barbaro but to herself, and turned on him angrily. 'I should have picked it up.'

'Get over the guilt and tell me what you remember.'

His sharp voice shook her into gear. 'It happened so gradually I hardly noticed.'

'Until you couldn't wake her, I presume? Has anything like this ever happened before?'

'Never.'

'This is important, Nell,' he warned.

'Do you think I don't know that? And it's Ms Foster, thank you.' She stared at him with hostility. But for Molly's sake she had to go over everything again. Nell started to snatch at whispery strands of recollection from the day—the simple breakfast, the cappuccino froth lodging on her lip, which Molly had wanted to copy…dabbing it on, holding her up to laugh at her reflection in the mirror… Nothing to give warning of what was to come. And why was he examining Molly's fingertips again? Was she getting worse?

The fear was rising again. It sat on her thought processes like a heavy weight. This was far worse than Jake's accident, even though she'd been pregnant with Molly then, and still had everything to learn about betrayal, loss and loss of trust. She had survived the disillusionment of discovering Jake's double life, survived having everything she believed in ripped away, and with no warning at all, but, staring at Molly lying lifeless in Luca's arms, she wasn't sure she was equal to this.

She wanted to ask more questions, but remembered from her experience with Jake that doctors were masters of deception. What would this man tell her that she could believe? She had been told so many lies. *Where there's life, there's hope*— that was just one of the many platitudes she had been fed in the hospital. No one told her before she went into Jake's room that he was already brain-dead, and that his body only lived on thanks to the machines breathing for him.

'Have you come up with anything yet?'

Dragging herself back to the present, Nell realised that Luca Barbaro had a frighteningly similar manner to the doctors she had encountered in the hospital following Jake's accident. 'I'm trying to remember.' She was struggling with every atom of intellect at her command to try and pin down a trigger. If she could just identify the moment when things had changed…

She'd been over and over it, and still nothing new, and now the past was sucking her down again like quicksand. Jake's death had flung back the curtain on his secret life, proving she hadn't known the man she loved, the man she believed loved her and their unborn child. But Jake was wild, a free spirit. He would never have been content with a conventional life with her…

Barbaro was staring at her, Nell realised, his eyes hypnotic, demanding. He'd guessed something was chipping away at her mind. She didn't want him climbing inside her head, reading her thoughts.

'Tell me everything you did from leaving the hotel,' Barbaro prompted.

His manner rankled. He was so sure of himself, so altogether comfortable in his deeply tanned skin. But however much she wanted to hit back, this was for Molly, and she would give him every bit of help that she could. 'She became sleepy about half an hour after we boarded the gondola. At first I thought it was because she found the ride soothing. I was day-dreaming too…' Nell stopped abruptly. Help was one thing, sharing her personal impressions with this man was something else.

'And before that?'

'Nothing. She was fine.'

'You're sure?'

'Of course I'm sure. Will you give her to me?'

'No. You might drop her.'

'Drop her?' Was he mad? 'I can assure you, I won't!'

'You look light-headed to me.'

'Is that in your professional opinion?'

Ignoring the sarcasm, he leaned out again, and so far this time, Nell grabbed him by the sleeve.

He looked down at her hand on his arm and she quickly drew it back.

'Will you please try to calm down?'

'How do you expect me to be calm when you take chances with my daughter—when you stand there saying nothing, explaining nothing?' Nell shook her head. She would never get through to him. As far as Dr Barbaro was concerned, she was the unavoidable encumbrance that came with each of his patients—their relative or friend.

Digging in her pocket, she found her phone. Relief flooded through her; she could do something now. She could ring the emergency services—take over. And the number was…?

Why hadn't she thought to ask at the hotel about the local emergency number? Because an emergency was the last thing you thought about on holiday...because all it took was one ray of sunshine and your brain shut down.

'What are you doing?' Luca Barbaro said sharply.

She ignored him and kept on punching numbers. 'I'm ringing our hotel.'

'Why?'

'To ask them for the number of the emergency services.'

'I'm perfectly capable of handling this. It's too late for them to do anything, and you'll just complicate everything. It will be quicker if we wait.'

'For how long?' she almost shouted.

'You'd make better use of your time if you could remember something.'

Their voices were rising over Molly's head, Nell realised, clamping her mouth shut. Did he think she was being deliberately obstructive?

'Where did you start your day?' he demanded.

She thought back to St Mark's Square: grandeur and scale beyond imagining. Pigeons wheeling over their heads like dull grey streamers. The cafés, the crowds. Molly eating ice cream, pasta... She blenched. 'Molly doesn't have food poisoning, does she?'

He frowned, but didn't answer.

'Don't you know?'

'I'm sorry, I'm not prepared to confirm or deny anything until I'm certain.'

He was sorry? She doubted that somehow. 'You must be able to tell me something.'

'I'm afraid I can't.'

She gritted her teeth. 'How far away are we from the hospital?'

'Not too far.'

'Then why don't we walk?' she said with exasperation.

'Not too far by boat,' he clarified.

Nell felt as if she was tearing up inside with frustration. She wanted to do something. Most of all, she wanted the ground to open up and swallow him, leaving Molly safe and well in her pushchair. With an angry sound she raked her hair.

'If this is getting too much for you, I could always help you down to that ledge and you could sit down.'

Too much for her? Sit down? She couldn't believe he was pointing to a seat cut into the rock beside the steps rubbed smooth by countless weary travellers—as if she could relax like them. 'I'm not tired!' She ignored his outstretched hand. The last thing she wanted to do was sit down. No, not the last thing. That had to be taking his hand. She had no intention of touching any part of him.

The black-gold gaze lingered on her face. 'Worrying will only sap your energy.'

'Thanks for the advice.' Nell raked her hair again until it stood in even angrier spikes. 'Why don't you save the platitudes, and give my daughter back to me?'

'Bad temper won't help either...'

He was looking at her hair. Let him look. It perfectly mirrored her feelings. Doubtless Barbaro preferred his women to have long, silky tresses he could wind around his fist...

A siren blasted and Nell exhaled with relief. At last something was happening.

The launch painted in orange and white had *Ambulanza* emblazoned along the side and across the front. Moving steadily towards them, it finally slowed beside the steps.

'Be careful when you climb on board,' Luca Barbaro advised. 'Leave Molly's pushchair to one of the men. We haven't time to deal with a second emergency.'

And then he was gone—with Molly. When she went to follow, one of the paramedics got in her way. Nell panicked, the past mocking her, reminding how they had kept her away from Jake. But then Barbaro stuck his head out of the cabin to see where she was and shouted something in Italian. She didn't wait to work out what it was. The man moved out of the way, and she hurried on board.

The fear that she would be separated from Molly was so real Nell had to ram the past back in its box and lock it up again. She had to tell herself that this wasn't a replay of Jake's accident, but something entirely different, and that she had to keep a clear head if she was going to stay on top of this new nightmare.

As she ducked her head to enter the cabin she could see Luca Barbaro was already treating Molly. He was clearly in his element, moving purposefully, calmly. The men knew him and watched him confidently. Their attitude relaxed her a little.

'Sit here, please.' Without taking his attention from Molly, Barbaro directed her to a bench seat on the opposite side of the cabin. As far away from Molly as possible.

He'd shifted up a gear, sloughing off all the irritation she'd sensed on shore. He was delivering instructions into his phone now, as well as to the men on board, and she didn't need to understand the language to know who was in charge, or to gather that this was a full-blown emergency and there was no time to lose.

The creeping cold that had started down her spine spread to Nell's shoulders as she sat watching. She didn't even know that she was shivering until Luca Barbaro turned in the middle of attending to Molly and murmured something to one of the paramedics. Then the man tossed a blanket over her shoulders and she drew it tight.

Nell watched him work with a mixture of awe and dread, all the time willing Molly to wake up. But it didn't take long for her to lose her flimsy faith. She was stung into speech by the sight of a syringe in his hand.

'Are you sure all this is necessary?'

'Yes.' He glanced over his shoulder too briefly to make eye contact.

She had only wanted him to explain what he was doing. He had checked Molly's vital signs, listened to her chest, checked her pulse, her blood pressure, tapped her back, scrutinised her fingernails for the umpteenth time and shone a light into her eyes. And now she wanted to be with Molly, holding her…

Nell made her request the moment he straightened up.

Barbaro remained staring at Molly, waiting for signs of improvement, she guessed.

'Not yet.'

'When?' But the powerful engines started up at that moment, drowning out her voice, and then the launch surged forward, fixing her in place. Nell waited until she judged it safe to move—

'Sit down!'

The harsh command shunted ice through her veins. She speared a look of resentment at him, but at that moment the launch picked up speed, and as it thrust forward the prow lifted, tilting the deck at an extreme angle. Thrown off balance, she was forced to make a grab for one of the upright poles and cling on desperately.

Barbaro's voice reached her over the roar of the engines. 'Police launches and ambulances break the speed limits inside the city and we'll be going even faster when we reach the Grand Canal. Get back to your seat and sit down now. It isn't safe to stand up.'

Tears of frustration welled in Nell's eyes. 'You might have warned me.' But Barbaro had already turned back to tend to Molly. She tried to get back to her seat, but the launch hit another boat's wake and lurched unexpectedly.

Nell finally staggered back to her seat, where the weight of emotion pinned her in place. Terror made her want to cry, to sob hysterically and shout out: why? Why Molly? The emotion building in her throat, in her chest was nearly choking her. She guessed that everyone on board would be used to emotional incontinence—all the more reason not to give way to it. She would hold herself in check—do whatever it took not to distract them from treating Molly. Her chest was heaving convulsively, but she made herself calm down. Then at last Dr Barbaro stood back and she could see Molly clearly.

Nell paled. There were so many tubes and wires connected to Molly's tiny frame. She stared up fearfully, trying to read Luca Barbaro's face, his eyes… She was so hungry for information. Why didn't he say something to her?

'Can I sit with Molly now?' Her voice was small. 'Can I hold her?'

'You might dislodge the drip.'

The drip? She hadn't noticed it before, but now she did. It was suspended above Molly like an abomination. 'I wouldn't—' Nell's throat seemed to be caught in a vice. 'Does she need that?'

'It's used for rehydration, and we're giving antibiotics too, as a precaution.'

Nell frowned. 'You don't know what's wrong with my daughter but you're pumping her full of drugs?'

'I consider it necessary.'

'And what's that machine?' She wanted to know. She wanted to know everything. She wanted to drive him, drive him hard. How else was she to find out what was going on? How else was she going to let him know she was there for Molly?

'A nebuliser. It delivers the medicine in a fine mist so the patient can breathe it in without it disturbing them.'

'Without it disturbing them?' Nell shuddered as she stared

at the mask on Molly's face, the coarse green elastic binding her fine baby hair to her moist skin. The noise from the machine was enough to disturb anyone. But that was the whole point, wasn't it? Nothing was going to disturb Molly; nothing could disturb her while she was in this condition.

The sooner they arrived at the hospital the sooner she could breathe easily again, Nell realised. Or maybe not even then. Maybe this man was representative of the type of cold-hearted individual she was going to find there. Something inside her said, if she could just touch Molly, give her love…

'I won't disturb her, and I won't pull anything out.'

She suffered his scrutiny in silence, holding herself together in the hope of passing his test.

'All right,' he agreed finally and, Nell guessed, reluctantly. 'I'll lift her onto your knee and then you can hold her while she inhales the medicine.'

'Thank you.' She was so grateful, all her feelings of hostility towards him started to fade. 'Does she need the drip as well as the mask?' Nell tried not to let her gaze linger on the fine tubing hanging from Molly's slender arm. Molly had never needed a plaster to cover an abrasion in her whole life, let alone required a needle to be inserted in her arm…

'It's the most efficient way I know to administer antibiotics and rehydrate the body.'

The body? Nell gasped involuntarily.

'Your daughter,' he corrected himself tersely.

Had she got through to him? His dispassionate voice suggested otherwise. 'The most efficient way *you* know? How can I be sure you know what you're doing?'

'You can't. I'll have to take her off you if you are going to get upset.'

'Don't threaten me! I've got no intention of breaking down, I can assure you,' she managed coldly, staring into his eyes until he looked away. Then she drank in every nuance of Molly's changed appearance. Rather than its usual porcelain perfection, Molly's complexion was ashen and her lips were tinged with blue…like her nails. She looked up again. 'I think it's time you told me what's going on.'

'When I know I'll tell you, and not before.'

He was not prepared to deliver a diagnosis that might be disproved once the child was admitted to hospital, where all the necessary tests could be carried out, nor was he accustomed to being harangued—let alone by some pixie-haired termagant with eyes like cobalt searchlights. He'd been looking forward to some hard-won down time when the call came through from Marco, the gondolier. He hadn't had chance to eat or to drink all day, let alone take a shower, or shave. And his reward for a being a good citizen? A woman who scrutinised his every move as if he were a first-year med student!

If the child hadn't been so sick he would have left her in the care of his very competent colleagues on board the ambulance. Then her mother could have driven *them* crazy with her questions. His focus was always on the people under his care. Relatives and friends were the province of his nurses. They acted as intermediaries for him, shielding him from distraction—just the way he liked it. If Nell Foster wanted more—well, she couldn't have it.

But something made him wonder about her backstory. Why had *Ms* Foster stripped every bit of feminine allure from her appearance? There wasn't a suggestion of femininity in her baggy clothes, and the spiky hair was a good indicator for her personality. Her face looked as though it had never seen make-up, and yet her eyebrows were beautifully shaped, and her eyes, fringed with long black lashes, were beautiful. Her teeth were film-star perfect—a fact he could attest to with confidence, since she drew back her lips to snarl at him as many times as most people cast deferential smiles in his direction.

Deferential, her? That was a laugh! She evidently hated doctors, mistrusted them…and him most of all. In this situation he would have expected her to be grateful, hanging on his every word, but she couldn't have made it plainer that she considered him to be a threat rather than a help to her daughter.

Nevertheless, she stirred feelings in him he was finding it hard to ignore. Her attitude irritated him, he was affronted by it, but there was something more, something electric… But those feelings were not only unusual for him, they were also forbidden to a man in his position. It was more than his fledgling career was worth to…

To what? Sleep with Nell Foster?

That was what he'd wanted to do since the first moment he'd set eyes on her—and therefore he had to put distance between them the moment he could.

CHAPTER THREE

'I'M STILL waiting for an explanation,' she reminded him.

He watched her glance sweep across the lines and tubes attached to his patient. Nell Foster was continually harassing him and questioning his judgement. Part of him resented it, part admired her spirit, but most of all he was concerned for the child lying so still and silent on the stretcher. He didn't want to show the mother how concerned he was. She was steadier now and he wanted to keep her that way. Too much knowledge would frighten her, too little might raise her hopes.

He found himself assessing her covertly. The mother was very different from the child. Nell Foster was robust, her features strong and clearly defined. It followed that the child must take after her father, which opened up more questions. He made himself stop and turn back to his charge. The little girl's eyes were as vividly blue as her mother's—he'd seen that when he checked her over. But was her gaze half as direct? He could only hope she was a fighter like her mother.

'I'm still waiting!'

He turned his professional face to Nell. Her wide, intelligent gaze assured him she wouldn't let up. It also hit him forcibly in the chest. Clearing his throat, he gazed at the roof of the cabin and launched into a reasonable explanation without giving too much detail. 'There's some congestion in your daughter's lungs. I'm trying to ease her breathing.' He stopped there, but even this was a first. He never divulged information piecemeal, never uttered a word that wasn't backed up by hard fact. There was a whole range of tests he would have to carry out before he could be sure of his diagnosis...

'When will you be able to give me some real answers?'

He had to look at her. 'Soon, I hope.'

'You hope?' She was scathing. 'How soon can we get someone else to look at Molly—someone who can do more than hope?'

Her mouth was set in a firm line, which drew his attention to her lips. He ignored the insult, and tried to ignore her lips. He brought professionalism to bear like a steel curtain, cutting Nell Foster out of the picture. 'At the very least, I'll need an X-ray to confirm my diagnosis. The drugs should help—'

'Should?'

'Medicine is not an exact science.' He couldn't believe how pompous he sounded.

'So why not leave her alone until we reach the hospital? Anyone can see she's sleeping. I think it would be better if you left her to rest rather than pumping her full of drugs before you know what you're doing!'

'Oh, do you?' He'd had enough, but bit his tongue and focused on the child lying on the stretcher. How could he tell Nell Foster that her daughter wasn't sleeping, but unconscious?

'If Molly is having difficulty breathing,' Nell persisted, 'we should be able to hear something. Coughing, wheezing.' Her eyes sharpened with certainty, and as he watched hope flood her face something rapped again on the stone he called a heart.

'Nell, stop this!'

He didn't know why he'd used her first name in such an emotional and unprofessional way, but the strange thing was that when Nell Foster's eyes filled with tears his stung too. And it was not just tiredness that made him empathise with his patient's mother—there was something more, something he had never let through before. There was fragility behind her bravado; he could hear it like a silent cry of desperation. 'It isn't always that simple,' he said carefully. Most people would be content with that.

He should have known. 'Go on,' Nell said, firming her jaw.

He looked at her and measured her strength. It didn't fall short, and that was something he could connect to. He owed it to her to be straight. 'Sometimes, when things are really serious, there's very little to hear at all.'

'Really serious?' She looked at him and he saw her spirit crumple; the fire went out of her, which again, incredibly, hurt him like hell.

What was this? What was happening to him? He never got involved emotionally. It was one of the first things he'd learned at med school—the moment you became prey to your emotions you were no use to anyone, least of all your patient. 'Try not to get upset.' He knew it sounded trite but he didn't know what to say, had never felt like this before. He longed to escape the suffocating tension swirling round the cabin.

'What do you suggest?' Her voice was shaking with emotion. 'Am I supposed to remove myself to some emotion-free zone when I've just been told my daughter is dangerously ill?'

He could think of nothing to say.

'Luca?' she pressed.

Her use of his first name gave him a jolt, even though he knew it was merely a measure of her desperation. 'We can only wait now,' he said honestly.

Did he really think she was going to crumble? Nell wondered, holding Luca's gaze. Maybe at one time in her life she might have broken down, but not now. The turning point had been Molly's birth. She'd had something to fight for since then. She would keep this vigil with him, keep it and will Molly well again.

Nell forced herself to look at everything dispassionately, to listen and become accustomed to all the alien sights and sounds: the nebuliser humming, the launch's engines throbbing, the muted Italian exchanges rising and falling expressively around her like a song.

'*Andiamo!*'

Luca barked out his instruction as they turned into the wide stretch of water that formed the main thoroughfare through Venice. It jolted Nell back to reality, made it hard to cling to the little life-raft of calm she had formed in her mind. She clutched the seat, ready now as the launch tipped at an even steeper angle. But the momentum jerked her forward and she was only stopped from slipping off the seat by Luca's whip-fast reactions.

'Sit back as far as you can, or I'll have to take her from you.'

His voice was as harsh as before. She had put too much store in the brief flash of kindness. Nell drew Molly closer. No one was going to take Molly from her. Her daughter was back where she belonged, where she was going to stay...

'Don't hold her so tightly.'

She loosened her grip immediately. She wanted to get it right for Molly.

'If you must lean on something, lean on me.'

Lean on him? 'I'd rather not.'

'Just until you become used to the rhythm of the boat—'

'I can manage, thank you!' Nell shrank away, relieved when Luca seemed to have second thoughts and left her to have a word with the captain of the boat, but even his back view was unsettling.

Dr Luca Barbaro was a manifestation of everything Nell knew she had to fear. He was arrogant, with an iron resolve, along with an innate certainty that everything he did or said was right. She took in the wide shoulders blocking out the light, the legs aggressively planted on the deck to keep him steady...the hands she could only describe as fighting, strong hands, but with a doctor's long, tapering fingers. Every square inch of the flesh she could see appeared to be tanned a uniform bronze. Luca Barbaro would have fit well in some medical drama played out on television—one where the lead doctor was improbable heartthrob material. She could only hope he possessed more qualifications than his Hollywood counterparts.

Nell tried to relax, tried to settle into the rhythm of the boat so that Molly would be comfortable. But her thoughts kept on colliding like skittles. How long before they reached the hospital? How long before they found a proper doctor? How long before someone told her what was wrong with Molly?

'I'll take her now.'

Had they arrived? Nell looked up and realised they had. As she started to get up Luca stopped her.

'I'll take her,' he repeated. 'She'll be safer with me.'

Safer? How could a child be safer anywhere than in its mother's arms? But there was such a tangle of wires and tubes hanging from Molly, Nell was terrified she might dislodge one of them.

Luca put his free hand on her shoulder and pressed her down. 'I want you to wait for one of the men to help you disembark. I live and work in Venice, so I'm used to travelling at high speed on water. You might be a little unsteady on your feet.'

She had vowed not to let Molly out of her sight, but what if she stumbled and hurt her in some way—pulled out one of the tubes?

As she watched them go, Nell suffered a presentiment; the

dark cloud enveloping her made her doubly impatient to disembark. 'Look after her,' she called.

Luca Barbaro didn't look back as he walked swiftly away with Molly and one of the paramedics at his side, holding the drip.

The men on board the launch seemed to take so long securing the mooring ropes, though it could only have been a matter of seconds, Nell reasoned, telling herself to be calm. She had no option but to wait until they had finished in order to have Molly's pushchair brought up from the hold. Meanwhile she followed Molly's progress on shore. There was a nurse waiting for the new patient outside the hospital gates. Luca didn't break stride as he drew level with the man; the only concession he made was to angle his head to accommodate the nurse's shorter frame as they exchanged information, and then they disappeared through some gates.

She was like a hare out of the traps when one of the crew finally came to help. But Luca had been right, and she was glad of the man's steadying hand as she left the launch. The swirling brown water looked far from inviting from this angle, and she couldn't adjust to terra firma right away.

'*Piano, piano, signora,*' the man insisted, holding on to her.

Nell claimed the pushchair, called her thanks and was off. It was as if Molly had left a burning trail, which if she hurried she was sure she could follow.

'*Signora?*' A security guard stood in her way.

'What do you want?' Nell knew she sounded impatient, and her voice was shaking, but Molly's trail was growing cold. 'I'm with Dr Barbaro.'

The guard stood firm.

'You have to let me go inside. Dr Barbaro has taken my daughter into the hospital.' She mimed, pointing, hoping he understood. 'You must have seen them? They were here just a minute ago. You have to let me pass!'

But the language barrier proved insurmountable. *'Signora, per favore…'*

'No! You have to let me in!' Her voice was desperate, and she tried to twist past him. But the security guard had seen it all and put his hand on the gate, stopping her.

'Mi dispiace…' Nell struggled to compose herself. 'I'm sorry.' She used her hands to make placating gestures while she racked her brain for some useful words. None would come. Her knowledge of Italian was so limited. She tried smiling—that always worked. 'I don't speak Italian, *signor.*' It was so hard trying to appear normal, rational, calm—the type of person a security guard would happily allow inside his hospital. Impossible, in fact, when the world and everything in it was swirling in front of her eyes and the only image she could see clearly was Molly lying in Luca Barbaro's arms. Molly attached to tubes and wires, Molly's beautiful face half-hidden by a mask. Molly. *'Per piacere, signore…'* Nell was nearly sobbing now.

'Mi dispiace, signora.' The guard shook his head.

'You *have* to let me in!' Nell tried brute force, her weight against his. 'I have a little girl to go to!'

But she had no chance of getting through. As her shoulders slumped in defeat, the guard cupped her elbow and gently chivvied her along to the door of his stone-built security post, which was situated on the wrong side of the hospital gates. Leaving her for a moment, he stepped inside his lodge and locked the door.

It had finally happened. Her worst nightmare had come true. Luca had taken Molly—shut her out when Molly needed her most.

Nell started in alarm as a small wooden panel slid open in front of her face.

'*In primo luogo, signora, dove fare questo—*'

'I must do what?' Nell gazed at the form in the security guard's hand with foreboding. 'Oh, no, *signor...*'

'*Si,*' he said firmly. '*Per favore.*'

A glance around the towering walls dividing her from Molly was all it took to convince Nell she had to comply. When he handed her the form she had to fill in Nell measured the sheets in one angry gesture. She had to fight for control. '*Un—er—biro, signor, per piacere?*'

'*Certo.*' With obvious relief he handed a pen over.

Nell raced through the form, interpreting it as best she could. Fortunately, forms the world over were much the same, and she did have some experience of filling them in, though she tried not to think about the last time she had done so. When she had finished the guard took them from her and checked each page meticulously.

'Can I go now?' It was like being back at school. Only she was older, and this wasn't playtime.

'*Si, signora.*' The guard pulled back from the opening.

His manner had changed to reveal more consideration. But she didn't want to dwell on the sympathy she could see in his eyes: she had to stay strong; she had to pay careful attention to his directions. She would forgive him anything if he would just hurry!

Nell abandoned the pushchair, and started to run.

The first corridor she came across was long and featureless. At the end she had two choices. Molly's trail had vanished. Nell stared from left to right and back again. Then in answer to her prayer a door opened.

'My daughter, *mia figlia...trauma...*?' Nell tried everything she could think of as the nurse came towards her.

'*La piccola raggazina?*'

'*Si!*'

The nurse put a hand on her arm, which Nell shook off angrily. The nurse seemed to understand, though, and smiled reassurance. 'This way, *signora*. Please, come with me.'

The nurse seemed so bright, so happy and confident. Nell told herself her manner had to be a sign that Molly must have recovered. She was even smiling expectantly as they walked through some swing doors into a treatment room. But the smell of antiseptic hit her, tossing her back into the nightmare of Jake's accident, and the lights were so bright…

As Nell began to orientate herself she felt the nurse's steadying hand creep beneath her arm.

Molly was lying propped up on a bank of pillows. Her tiny arms were like sticks at either side of her body, her tiny fists digging into the mattress as if she was struggling to hold herself even more erect in order to breathe. Was she awake? It was impossible to tell.

For the first time since this whole dreadful episode had started Nell found she was hoping Molly wasn't. She didn't want her to be awake while her fragile blue-veined chest was pumping frantically. She looked in agony, and the strain on her heart had to be enormous.

Slowly Nell's focus expanded to take in the nurse standing at each corner of the bed. Luca was standing at the head of it, closest to Molly. He turned as if he had been expecting her.

'There's nothing more you can do?' She guessed that much and then thought his lips looked dry. She noticed that he had to moisten them with his tongue before he could answer.

'No.'

She waited, but that was all he said. Without waiting to be invited Nell went straight to Molly's side. Kneeling on the floor, she took her daughter's hand and pressed it to her cheek. Then the miracle she been hoping for happened. Opening her eyes, clutching at her throat, Molly turned her head.

'Mumma,' she gasped.

CHAPTER FOUR

'No! You can't ask me to go there. I hate Venice! I'm never going back! Not even for the sake of the organisation...'

That was what she'd said to her committee, Nell remembered, yet here she was, speaking in Venice to introduce the hospital patients' support charity she had founded almost ten years before. The cause she believed in so passionately was far more important than any personal considerations.

She'd had plenty of practice and was a seasoned public speaker, but even so she was nervous tonight. Nowhere made Nell quite so tense as Venice, with its stylish inhabitants and bitter memories. And although only one doctor was holding out against her scheme, he was influencing everyone else. He was Medical Director of his family's hospital trust, the man the rest looked to for their lead—the man she had to convince if this hospital was to be the flagship to spread her scheme across Venice and then Italy, as they had planned. Nell was the scheme's founder, the one who could persuade the obstinate Medical Director to get the ball rolling. So, here she was. Shaking.

The moment she had been told the name of the doctor she had to convince, a face had flashed into her head. She had tried to deny the possibility that it was the same man, telling herself that the Dr Barbaro she'd met would have moved on by now. Barbaro was a popular surname in Italy, and 'her' Luca Barbaro belonged to the past, along with Molly's nightmarish and thankfully only truly serious asthma attack.

It had taken time to confirm. Asthma wasn't easy to be sure of in a very young child. But he'd been sure, Nell remembered. Luca Barbaro had been sure of his diagnosis and had put her in touch with the very best specialist in the field, a man who would continue the investigations he had started when they returned home.

A lot of things had changed since then, Nell thought, viewing her face critically in the mirror. She'd known that if she wanted to win people over she had to inspire confidence. The first thing to go had been her spiky hair. She smiled as she started brushing out her shoulder-length bob. It was hard to believe she had once sported such a radical hairstyle and boho clothes.

She was especially glad to be wearing her confidence-inspiring uniform today. She needed it more than the audience! The crisp white shirt, dark business suit and low-heeled courts formed a suit of armour she could hide behind.

She wasn't going to let the past—any part of it—interfere with the project that was so dear to her. But she knew at least some of the adrenaline racing through her veins was for the memory of the man who had stood so squarely against her in Venice. Enough time had passed for her to be able to separate Luca Barbaro the man from Luca Barbaro the doctor tending Molly—and the man had left a lasting impression.

Nell's face lit up as her thoughts switched to her boisterous ten-year-old. Molly was here with her now in Venice. Some of Jake's insurance money had been used to employ the very best nanny Nell could find, an older woman called

Marianna, who travelled everywhere with them. The three of them lived a simple life, with no men to complicate the situation. Living without romance had proved easier than Nell had imagined. The most important thing was that Molly had consistency in her life. She would not risk some man breezing into their lives then breezing out again. She had better things to think about.

Nell sensed Molly's approach before she even heard her daughter's footsteps. Just as on every other day, she spared a moment to give thanks for Molly's continued good health and by the time the door burst open, she was standing in front of it with her arms spread wide in invitation. As Molly flung herself into Nell's embrace, it was hard to imagine that this was the child who had been taken so gravely ill the last time they had visited Venice.

She had Barbaro to thank for that, Nell reflected. And yes, perhaps she had been guilty of underestimating him at the time. But she had been so strung out, and had thought him too young to deal with such a critical situation. It was largely thanks to him Molly had recovered, that she was able to live a normal life and engage in every activity a child of her age was entitled to enjoy.

His parting letter to them had been brief but detailed and Nell could remember her surprise when she'd received it. She still resented the way he'd walked out on them both without a backward glance the instant Molly was moved into the children's ward. They hadn't seen him again, not once—his letter had been handed to her by a nurse. But she still kept a log of Molly's symptoms as he had advised, and ensured Molly received careful monitoring under the supervision of the doctor Luca Barbaro had recommended.

Nell tried to blank her mind to the dark eyes haunting her thoughts. Luca Barbaro's lack of human consideration still had the power to sting. But it was his arrogant manner together with the aftermath of Jake's accident that had propelled her work forward, so it had done some good.

Hearing Molly chatting happily with Marianna now made Nell angry all over again on her daughter's behalf. What kind of cold-hearted individual lost interest in his patient the moment the crisis was over? She had expected a few words at least for Molly, even perhaps some acknowledgement for herself—she wasn't sure why or of what, just that she'd wanted something from him. But he'd simply handed them over to the care of his nursing team, written a brief letter and disappeared.

That was years ago. She was over it now, and having Molly with her in Venice had transformed the dreaded return into fun. No one was going to spoil that for them. As far as Nell was concerned they were laying the final ghost together. And now it was almost time for the meeting to start. She had to forget Barbaro and concentrate on that.

'Ready?'

Nell smiled as Marianna asked the question. 'As I'll ever be. Come with me for luck, Molly?'

'Can I sit in the audience when you go onto the platform?'

'Of course. Marianna, could you stay with her?' Nell was used to imposing her will these days, but never on a woman she considered to be almost a surrogate mother to them both.

'I wouldn't miss it for the world,' Marianna assured her.

The first few seconds of any talk were always the worst. After that Nell always settled into her stride. Today was different. Today, as she delivered her prepared talk, Nell was conscious of two things: Molly and Marianna creeping down the steps at the side of the platform to find a seat near the front…and a man standing at the back of the room in the shadows.

Nell felt him even before she saw him, and her heart raced in response. From that moment on, his presence was a nagging distraction. The lights had been dimmed to allow the audience's attention to focus on the stage, but through some inner eyes she could sense his every movement—the regular movement of his chest as he drew breath, the muscle working in his jaw… She tried to tell herself that she was being ridiculous, but unless Luca Barbaro had a *doppelgänger* in Venice, there was no mistaking the arrant masculine figure.

It was her worst nightmare come true. It was also her moment of triumph, Nell told herself firmly. Each time one of her volunteers went into a hospital to speak up for anxious relatives, she thought of Luca Barbaro and the offhand way he had treated them—leaving her at the mercy of a security guard while Molly was taken away, refusing to give her any information about Molly's condition… His lack of consideration was one of the prime drivers that had led her to expand the scheme—a fact she was sure he would be delighted to learn.

Firming her jaw, Nell continued with her speech. There would have to be a meeting with Barbaro at some point, she knew that, but she had thought it would be conducted somewhere different, somewhere private—a sterile office, neutral territory, where she would lay her case before him with the same lack of passion he had displayed the first time they met. But for this one evening this hall was her territory, and the man in the shadows was a hostile and unwanted intruder who had chosen not to sit with the rest of the audience, but to remain leaning against the door with his arms folded across his chest as if to signify the fact that he wasn't going anywhere. And even with a roomful of people between them she could sense his animosity.

A *frisson* of alarm ran down Nell's spine when he shifted position. He was even taller than she remembered, and the heat of his stare was drilling into her…

She had stopped talking, Nell realised; everyone was waiting for her to continue. With a quick smile of reassurance, she started to wind up her speech. She couldn't afford to lose her concentration now that she was about to throw the meeting open to questions.

She had made sure that invitations had been delivered to every hospital and clinic in the area, not just the staff of this hospital in which she hoped to pilot the Venice scheme. The work of her volunteers depended upon the co-operation of the staff within each establishment…and that meant every single member of staff. Nell glanced again at the figure in the shadows, wondering what it would take to get Luca Barbaro on her side.

She listened carefully to each question, judging the mood of the audience before she spoke. She had less to do at the sharp end these days than she would have liked, but she was a good speaker, and her role was to spread the scheme, recruit and train. It was up to her to convince the audience that the successful record of her project was something they wanted to buy into.

For about a quarter of an hour things went really well. Nell was using an interpreter and the discussion so far had been good-humoured. It augured well for her pilot scheme. She was relieved to have found an answer to every question…relieved that the man in the shadows seemed to have disappeared.

'Will you personally set up your project?'

Every fibre in her body tensed. The voice, speaking English, was unmistakable.

'Yes.' Nell took a moment before saying anything more. Her breathing had turned instantly ragged, and she knew that her voice would be trembling when she spoke again if she didn't pull herself together. The last thing she wanted was for Luca Barbaro to know how badly he affected her.

'That's right, I will be staying in Venice while we test the pilot scheme.' She spoke firmly, scanning the room. But he had moved. The lights had been turned up for the questions, but she couldn't spot him. 'I always remain on call during the start-up period.'

The interpreter began to translate, which gave Nell the chance to search for Luca.

'So you're going to be working in the hospital, supervising the scheme?'

Nell ground her jaw. Why couldn't she see him? 'No, I'll be off site. My job is to train—'

'And to pass on your dislike and mistrust of the medical profession?'

Nell froze. She wasn't alone in that. Quite a few members of the audience had no trouble understanding English and she could hear a low rumble of surprise. When the interpreter translated Luca's words into Italian the rumble grew.

Everyone was waiting to see what she had to say in reply. She kept it light and friendly, even faintly indulgent, hoping to make it seem that she was dealing with an honest mistake, rather than a troublemaker. 'I'm sorry, but you're wrong, Dr…' She waited for Luca to supply his name—to come out of the shadows and face her like a man.

He chose not to.

Resting her hands lightly on the podium, Nell smiled ruefully at her audience. 'I couldn't do the work I do if I held those views, could I?'

'Really?' he demanded, and she saw him.

Luca Barbaro had moved into the centre aisle at the front of the stage in full view of everyone. 'I'd like to know how you expect to foster good relations between medical professionals and your organisation,' he went on, 'when you are so clearly suspicious and biased against—'

'Dr Barbaro, please.' Nell's voice rang out, silencing him. This wasn't the first time she'd been interrupted since founding the charity, and she had learned how to defuse most situations.

'*Signor* Barbaro,' the interpreter at her side discreetly corrected her. '*Signor* Barbaro is the medical director and one of the most eminent paediatric consultants in Venice.'

Nell made a thoughtful sound to show that she had heard. So Luca was right at the top of his profession—why wasn't she surprised? 'Signor Barbaro,' she continued smoothly, 'most facilities are only too happy to welcome our volunteers, and find that their work improves relations between patients, relatives and staff. I can assure you that you have nothing to fear from introducing our scheme in your hospital.'

Everyone in the hall must have heard his contemptuous huff. Nell's eyes hardened briefly, but then with a sweeping gesture she introduced the men and women sitting in a block in front of her. 'You can speak to any member of the team if you need more information on how we work. Most of these volunteers are in fact retired doctors or other members of the medical profession themselves.' Her trump card. Nell waited patiently for the interpreter to do her work.

'I'll speak to them as you suggest,' Luca agreed when the buzz of interest faded. 'And then I'll speak to you.'

He bowed, and the audience, reassured, started to applaud.

Gathering up her papers, Nell left the stage. She hoped to slip away, delaying the inevitable face-to-face encounter with Luca until she'd had time to prepare, but he was waiting for her at the foot of the steps.

'Hello, Nell. Welcome back.'

'Thank you.' Her heart was thundering so violently she could hardly breathe. She wasn't sure why he had attacked her in the hall, though she had swiftly defused it and he hadn't come back at her. 'It's been a long time.' She couldn't allow any of this to become personal. She was in Venice for a reason. Luca Barbaro's endorsement was crucial if her pilot scheme was to be a success.

But it didn't help that the response she'd had to him the first time they met hadn't faded. In fact it had hit home even more strongly, like a sledgehammer, making it impossible to think straight. It wasn't that he was older, or that his aura of power had increased…she wasn't sure what it was, but she knew that he affected her more urgently. He even smelled different: warm, spicy, masculine, dangerous…

'So, what brings you here? What makes you think Venice is in need of your services?'

He was like a coiled spring. She launched into her reassuring spiel. 'People everywhere welcome the support of our volunteers…'

This wasn't the right time or place for a serious discussion, though. 'Perhaps we can organise a proper meeting so that I can reassure you.'

'Perhaps…'

She didn't like the way he was looking at her—eyes darkening with something. Humour, maybe? Or rather, she liked it too much. She held his gaze because he had to know the strength of her resolve. This was a good scheme. It had helped more people than he could imagine, and she wouldn't let it fail because of the way this man made her feel.

He had more presence than she remembered. The planes of his face were more rugged and his hair had been cut abrasively short, which suited him. It suited the hard expression that had crept into his eyes. Everything about him was unsettling. The blue-black stubble was darker, the lips crueller but also more sensuous. He exuded strength and purpose and, she saw, an implacable resistance.

'How do you fund this?' he said bluntly.

Nell's hackles rose. Did he think she was dishonest? She didn't want to get into detail now, but she didn't want him running away with the thought that this was a profit-making exercise either. 'Donations, mostly. We're a registered charity. The volunteers work for expenses only, and some of them refuse to take even that. I am not salaried. I fund myself from an invested sum.' She stopped there, her eyes telling him plainly that was all he needed to know about her personal finances. She wasn't about to tell him it was the very large compensation pay-out she had received after Jake's death that had allowed her to start the scheme.

'This meeting wasn't about raising funds, *Signor* Barbaro.' Nell exaggerated his elevation just enough to let him know it gave him no greater standing in her eyes. 'It was about informing the local hospitals and the public about what we can offer. And may I remind you,' she continued evenly, 'that this isn't an ego trip for me, or for you? We're here to support people who need our help—and that's your help *and* mine.'

'As far as I'm aware, I'm already helping just by doing my job.'

Nice to know the ego was intact! 'But now we have a chance to do something together...' She broke off abruptly. Her usual line of persuasion hardly seemed appropriate in this instance.

'To do something together?' Luca prompted ironically.

She met his gaze without a flicker of expression. 'Yes, we would be working together for a time if you agree to let us set up the pilot scheme in your hospital.' She glanced around dismissively. 'Are there any more questions I can help you with now?'

'Just one. Who zipped you into that suit?'

The fact that he had noticed at all threw her—but then her

image had changed rather dramatically since the last time they had met. Even so, it was an uncomfortably intimate observation, and he had obviously meant it as a parting shot because by the time she was ready to fire back, he had started to walk away. 'Any more *sensible* questions?' she called after him.

He turned to stare at her over his shoulder, his lips tugging down in a wry smile as he pretended to reflect. 'No, I don't think so.'

'Good!' She snapped the word before she could stop herself, knowing she too was making it personal.

Luca's response was a long, slow smile, which reminded her how good he was at reading thoughts. 'But I'll be sure to think of some by the time we have our private meeting. Just you and me.'

Nell didn't know whether to be relieved or not when he walked away.

She didn't move until he had disappeared into the crowd and then she let out the air in her lungs in one juddering breath. She almost fell into the chair Marianna was holding out for her when she got back to the dressing room.

'Who was that?' Marianna's voice was a cautious mix of concern and suppressed excitement.

'You noticed?' Nell shrugged wryly.

Molly provided a welcome distraction, launching herself at Nell. 'You were great, Mum! And so was that man.'

'What man?' Nell's heart started thumping again. She knew very well to whom Molly was referring. 'What on earth makes you say that?'

'He made it exciting. Everyone shot up when he spoke.'

Nell's eyes narrowed as she caught Molly sharing a conspiratorial glance with Marianna. She'd make Barbaro shoot up next time she saw him...

The thought was barely formed before the door swung open.

'Hello again, Nell.'

Nell couldn't believe her eyes. She couldn't believe Luca would have the nerve to walk in unannounced. Her pulse was so far off the scale she couldn't even speak.

Molly spoke for her. 'Hello.' Tipping her head, she looked at Luca then at her mother, her eyes bright at the thought of the entertainment to come.

Luca hunkered down to Molly's level to introduce himself. 'Hi. So you're Molly.'

As Molly turned a questioning face her way Nell felt all the old resentment bubbling up inside her.

'Do you remember me, Molly?' Luca said.

'Of course I do. You called out to Mum when she was speaking in the hall.'

As Luca glanced around, Nell knew they were both thinking the same thing—the emergency hospital admission had left no imprint on Molly's young mind.

'Yes, that was rude of me.' He spoke casually, as if he and Molly were sharing a confidence.

'It made things interesting,' Molly observed. Her voice was neutral, but her glance kept flicking between Luca and her mother.

'It certainly did,' Luca agreed.

Nell didn't pick him up on it. She didn't want to make too much of what had happened in the hall for all sorts of reasons—most importantly, she didn't want Molly becoming suspicious.

Suspicious? There was nothing for Molly to become suspicious about. But she was clearly waiting for an explanation as to why they had such an interesting visitor.

Nell had made sure that Molly understood her condition for her own safety. They never laboured it, but there was no reason not to tell her about the first time they had met Luca.

'When you were taken ill in Venice all those years ago, Signor Barbaro was your doctor.'

'Oh, now I see.' Molly stared at Luca with increased interest.

'So, we're friends?' Luca held out his hand.

'You bet!' Molly's face broke into a grin.

The sight of the two of them forging a compact made Nell uncomfortable. But she was bound as always by her wish to put the project before her own feelings. And this meant that he was serious about them having a meeting. 'What can I do for you?'

'Thought I'd better tie up our appointment before you found yourself completely booked up,' he said. 'Five minutes of your time?'

'Of course.' Nell hadn't thought it would be so easy, but against all her expectations it seemed that Luca Barbaro was prepared to consider her scheme.

Marianna said, 'Don't forget our challenge back at the hotel, Molly.' Nell realised that she was about to take Molly and discreetly slip away. That she didn't want. 'You don't have to go.'

'Doom Merchant Seven,' Molly was confiding to Luca. 'Marianna will never beat me. I've reached level twelve.'

Luca dipped his head in approval. 'One short of me.'

'Really?' Molly's face was incandescent with admiration.

'Perhaps I'll take you on some time,' Luca suggested, standing up.

'Would you?'

Luca was probably just saying it for effect, Nell told herself, which Molly wouldn't realise. She would help him to back out gracefully and save Molly's feelings in the long run too. 'I'm sure *Signor* Barbaro has other things to do than play computer games.' Luca slanted her a glance, and she added sharply, 'Doubtless, as the top paediatric consultant in Venice and the medical director here, you have very little time to spare.'

He had moved behind her, where Molly could see him and she couldn't, though she could feel his warm breath brush her ear when he started speaking.

'You don't know me at all if you think I would pass up an opportunity to play Doom Merchant Seven with a master.'

Molly started giggling and Nell felt her face heat up. Luca was right. She didn't know him. Better for all of them if she kept it that way.

Marianna held out her hand. 'Come on, Molly, your mother's got things to talk about.'

'No!' Nell began to collect her things. 'Wait a minute and I'll come with you.'

'Why don't you come on later when we've finished our game?' Molly piped up. 'You'll only be bored sitting there watching us.'

Nell saw a muscle twitch in Luca's jaw and suspected he was trying not to laugh.

He waited until the door closed behind Molly and Marianna before saying, 'You're not frightened of me, are you, Nell?' He leaned back against the wall to stare at her, arms folded.

'Don't be ridiculous.' But what was ridiculous was the shimmer of desire quivering down her spine. 'What do you want?' An appointment, Nell wondered, or something more?

He tipped his head, his lips curving in a half-smile. 'You have nothing to fear from me. Weren't those your words to me back in the hall?'

'I might have said something like that with regard to the scheme,' Nell admitted. Tilting her chin, she held his gaze. 'No, I'm not scared of you. You're just here to make an appointment.'

'That's right. We didn't settle on a date or a time in the hall.' He smiled. 'I'd like to pin you down right now.'

CHAPTER FIVE

GRABBING her diary, Nell briskly settled on a mutually convenient date, then stowed the book back in her briefcase and made for the door. Business was one thing, lingering with Luca was another—and she had no intention of giving him the impression that her life was an open playing field.

Luca smiled to himself. She was tougher now, and far more together than he remembered, but brittle too. Maybe she would crack if he went in too hard. But maybe that was what he wanted. He might support her scheme, he might not... He'd need to know a lot more about it first. Like, how far would Ms Foster be prepared to go to gain his compliance?

OK, that wasn't one of the questions he'd be asking, but if she'd been a threat in those boho clothes with her hair gelled up in spikes, in a severe suit with her shirt buttoned up to her chin she was more of a promise. A promise he was making right now to himself. And that hair was glorious—how could she have ever cut it short? It looked as if every strand had been hand-polished with silk. How would it feel to run his fingers through it...how would it look spread out on a pillow?

'I won't keep you.'

He refocused. She was ending the meeting on him? Still, he liked a challenge. 'I think we've made a bad start.'

She didn't cave in right away at his admission, merely nodded and smiled gravely. He smiled too and turned up the charm. 'How about I buy dinner to make up for it?'

Her eyes widened as she stared at him. 'Dinner? Are you serious?'

'Why not?' He shrugged, lips pressing down as if everything in the hall had been nothing more than a misunderstanding. 'You asked for questions, I gave you questions. That's it. But I would like to discuss the scheme further.' Now he had to hope the project came before her pride.

As he waited for her response, he took the opportunity to observe her without distraction. It had been a long time and there were many changes. He always listened to his senses—how a patient looked, how they felt beneath his hands. His intuition had never let him down in the past and it was as acute as ever now. She was undeniably sincere about this scheme of hers—and though she obviously didn't know it, she was hot.

'Why are you smiling?'

Because she was different? Because he was intrigued, wanted to know all there was to know about her? No. Because this time he was going to take her to bed.

'Are you so confident I'll accept your invitation that you're already celebrating?' she suggested.

He killed the smile, ignored her cynicism and gave himself a sharp reminder that he couldn't afford any more lapses of attention. 'No, of course not.' He met the level gaze head-on. 'What on earth would I have to celebrate if you decided to accept?'

She smiled at that, almost. It made him feel good inside. Better than good. He had never forgotten her—had never forgotten the fright she had given him when he was just starting out on his career and the smallest indiscretion might have brought the whole pack of cards tumbling down. He'd been forced to remove himself from the case, but that didn't mean he'd forgotten Nell. When he'd heard she was coming to Venice he'd moved heaven and earth to make sure he could attend the meeting. And the moment he'd first set eyes on her again, the engine inside him had gone into overdrive. He'd had no alternative but to stand up, stand out, confront her, be the leader of the pack—there was a primeval instinct driving him. It wasn't her scheme he was arguing for or against; he was staking his claim.

Seeing Nell with Molly had complicated things. He had anticipated meeting up with the same harridan who had bad-mouthed the colleagues he held in such high regard, who thought all doctors were demons and who was asking to be thoroughly and relentlessly bedded until she became a recognisable human being. What he'd actually found was a dedicated worker on a crusade to improve the world, a mother whose whole face lit up every time she looked at her child…a woman with enough secrets hidden beneath that bright blue stare to pique his interest.

Plan 'A' had called for the briefest of introductions followed by consummation. Plan 'B' called for something rather more subtle—like dinner first, Venetian-style.

'In that case, I accept.'

'I beg your pardon?' For a moment he wondered what she was talking about. His senses were stirring all over the place, but the activity hadn't reached his brain yet.

'Dinner?' she reminded him. 'Now I know how much it will pain you to take me out, I couldn't possibly refuse. And you should pay a penance for your bad behaviour in the hall.'

A penance? He had to kill the thoughts darting round his head or she'd see them in his eyes and change her mind fast.

'Dinner together.' He affected a frown. 'Was that my idea?' It was fun provoking her, fun seeing her head cock to one side and her lips falling open in surprise...but the best fun of all was to be had seeing her eyes darken as she stared up at him.

'I believe so,' she observed primly. 'It certainly wasn't my idea. And I hope you'll be taking me somewhere nice—no fast food.' She raised a brow.

'Fast food?' He lingered over the words, if only because it gave him more time to look at her, to watch her blue eyes darkening still further. 'Only tourists eat on the run. A true Venetian likes to take his time and savour every mouthful.' *The same way he likes to make love.* But he didn't add that.

'I'm looking forward to it,' she said drily.

You and me both. He smiled faintly.

'It will be a good opportunity for me to have a preliminary chat with you about how our scheme can operate in your hospital before we have our actual meeting,' she went on, determinedly businesslike. 'I can assure you it has the potential to enhance the services you offer—'

'My services?' He kept his face perfectly straight.

'You are in charge now, aren't you?'

'Yes, I am.' Her eyes had changed—hardened—as she pursued her goal. He didn't want to get into discussions about business—not until he had investigated Ms Foster's personal potential a little further. 'I'm sure we'll find plenty of time to discuss your scheme over dinner.' He smiled reassuringly.

He sensed she hadn't forgiven him yet for his attack on her in the hall. He wasn't going to have it all his own way; they were well-matched. That made an exciting change.

'Venice will be our first outpost in Italy,' she remarked. 'Shall we go?'

He held the door for her. 'You're very sure of yourself.'

'I have to be if I'm going to support my team as they deserve, if I'm going to convince people like you that it's a good thing we're doing, and not a threat.'

He couldn't help but admire her control after the way he had gone for her in the hall. He also sensed she had softened towards him, if only because she could see a gleam of hope that he might be persuaded to consider allowing her volunteers into his hospital. He pressed home the advantage. 'I hope you're hungry?'

'Starving, Luca.'

The comic look was clearly meant to warn him she was going to eat her way through the menu, but her use of his first name was a definite plus...

'Signor Barbaro?' She waved her hands in front of his eyes as they stood waiting for the lift. 'Are you still with me?'

'You called me Luca—shall we stay with that?' He guessed she was balancing the need to get him on her side against her wish to keep him at a safe distance.

'All right. I suppose in that case you'd better call me Nell.'

He didn't point out that he usually did, but decided to make her work. 'I'm looking forward to discussing the project— though of course, if it's not convenient to have dinner now, Nell, we can make it some other time.' He made his voice uninterested, as though she'd lost his attention.

'No! No, dinner is great. I'll just call Marianna to let her know where I am, but that's fine.'

She sounded really worried as the lift doors slid open...and she trembled beneath his hand when he touched her back.

'Guess I'm stuck with you, then,' he said lightly.

She was as casual as could be, but she removed herself from touching distance once they were inside the lift. 'I guess you are.'

Luca Barbaro was the most charismatic human being she had ever met. She was in real danger of falling under his spell, Nell realised. How was she supposed to stop thinking what it would be like to be in bed with him?

Ever since she had discovered the truth about Jake she had stayed clear of sex. She'd got her fingers badly burned trying to hold the interest of a man every woman wanted—but now, thanks to Luca, her hormones were running riot again. Luca Barbaro was everything Jake had been, and much more. And now she was about to do business with a man who looked as if he might throw her to the ground and ravish her at the slightest provocation.

Was she ready for this? Blood surged through her veins as she thought about it. She had never felt so aware, so alive—which was all Luca's fault. Celibacy had been a piece of cake before he arrived on the scene.

'Nell?'

Nell's face flooded with heat as if he had guessed at all the erotic thoughts crowding her mind. And all he was doing was standing outside the lift doors waiting for her to step into the lobby.

'Shall we?' he invited.

She stepped out promptly, knowing she had to get him on board; if she did that, the rest would follow. She would have to chant that like a mantra if she was going to get through the rest of this evening unscathed.

Luca had chosen the very place Nell had been longing to try, though she had ruled it out, as it was far too expensive. It was small and smart, with leaded glass windows, and the sign above the door was discreet to the point of invisibility. It would have been almost impossible to find without him. Located in the maze of narrow walkways that spread out like a web behind the Grand Canal, it was reputed to have the best food in Venice. The concierge at the hotel had told her that even out of season a table had to be booked at least one month in advance. She noticed Luca didn't seem to have any trouble getting a table just by walking in off the street.

'A café would have been fine.'

Luca ignored that comment as he held her chair. 'Are you happy for me to order the food for you?' he said, once they had sat down.

'Perfectly.' It gave her a chance to weigh him up while he scanned the menu. 'But no tentacles, or stomach linings.'

'I'll see what I can do for you.'

Again the wry smile that made her heart pound, and his position a mere arm's length across the table from her was distinctly worrying. She should have thought more carefully before accepting this invitation.

He spoke rapidly to the waiter, who hurried back to the kitchen.

'What did you say?' she demanded. It had taken Luca all of five seconds to order their meal. Maybe it would just be one course and coffee? Perhaps he didn't want to linger over it either?

'The chef knows what's good. I've left it to him. Fish OK? I told him white fish, no awkward bones.'

'Not eel?'

He gave her a quizzical glance. 'Not very adventurous, are you, Nell?'

'I can be,' she said defensively.

'Plenty of adventure in other areas?' Luca suggested drily.

Arousal ripped through her like a tornado. There was a smile hovering around his lips, which warned her to be more circumspect about her assertions in future. It was easy to believe Luca knew every salacious thought running through her mind. And this was just a preliminary business meeting?

'Just no taste for slimy things,' she clarified, dragging the conversation back to terra firma.

Luca's smile deepened. 'But eel is delicious. Rich and savoury. And don't they say you should challenge yourself every day?'

'Well, this is my day off.'

'Really? I didn't know you had such a thing as a day off. In that case—'

'It's still a no-eel day,' she said, doubling her determination not to be drawn into a flirtatious discussion.

'That leaves us with a lot more avenues to explore…'

'Dead ends?' She firmed her lips. She mustn't get into verbal jousting with him! Easing her position on the seat, she picked up the discarded menu and started to study it avidly—until Luca took it out of her hands and replaced it the right way up.

The food came in a steady stream—asparagus spears dripping in butter, celery with olive oil, artichokes with parsley and mint, as well as delicious fat tomatoes sitting on a bed of finely chopped basil and mozzarella cheese. 'I'll never be able to eat a main course after this,' she moaned.

'Mangiando, mangiando, viene l'appetito.'

'I beg your pardon?' Nell paused with the fork halfway to her mouth.

'Something my grandmother used to say,' Luca explained. 'Eat, and your appetite will come.'

She didn't think he was talking about food.

The possibility of seeing more of Luca while she was in Venice was suddenly a very exciting prospect indeed…

No, Nell told herself firmly, she was being ridiculous. Maybe Luca was irresistible, but she wasn't the type to indulge in a holiday romance. She had too much responsibility to be able to disengage her everyday life from the possibilities that opened up when you were a stranger in a foreign country…

'Are you enjoying yourself, Nell?'

Actually no, she was feeling far too tense now. 'The food's

delicious,' she said carefully. It occurred to her then that beautiful people expected every door to open for them before they even had time to raise their fist and knock. Day-dreams were one thing, but she had to show Luca that her own door had no intention of opening for him—by so much as a crack.

Fat pink prawns slicked in butter and oil were followed by pasta in cream sauce, crisp slices of pizza, aromatic soup. 'Oh, no, really, not for me,' Nell protested as the waiter placed a plate of succulent melon and *prosciutto* ham in front of her.

'Don't you like it?' Luca frowned. 'I could have it changed for something else.'

'No, it's not that, but...'

'You can't eat any more?'

'I like to think I know when I've had enough.'

His lips curved as he inclined his head. 'That's good, Nell. Shall we take a pause? Another glass of wine, perhaps?'

'Half,' she cautioned.

As if he'd picked up her discomfort, he started talking about Molly, which was the verbal equivalent of a neck massage. At some time during the conversation the memory of him heckling her at the meeting faded into insignificance. Nell liked nothing more than to talk about Molly, and she was the one thing they had in common that was a safe topic. She explained how Molly's steady return to good health had given her the opportunity to expand the scheme—leaving out the part where Luca had been one of the drivers with his arrogance and aloofness.

'It's wonderful to hear,' he said. 'Some children can be lucky, others less so.'

'The diary helped a lot,' Nell admitted. The log of Molly's symptoms had been the prime instrument in keeping Molly's doctors accurately informed about her progress under their treatment.

'Do you still keep it?'

'Every day.'

'I'd like to see it some time.'

Nell was surprised to find it easier to talk to Luca now that he had slipped into professional mode. Was it possible he had moved on as much as she had? Was it too much to hope that, just as she had listened to his advice regarding Molly's treatment, Luca had taken note of her distress at being kept out of the information loop when Molly had been a patient in his hospital? Did it signal the fact that he really was receptive to her scheme?

'Never become complacent, will you?' He reclaimed her attention.

'Don't worry, I won't. And…'

'And?' he prompted.

'And thank you,' she said simply.

'It's my job,' he reminded her.

It was like crossing a bridge from her side to his. The vast chasm that had been between them had narrowed considerably, though it seemed strange to be thanking him when she had left Venice that first time so full of anger and resentment—feelings so pronounced she had built up her campaign on the strength of them.

'I've been thinking about what your organisation has to offer.'

Nell's ears pricked up. This was everything she had hoped for. It made dinner less of an ordeal as she struggled to keep her senses in check, and more of an opportunity.

Luca ordered water and they kept on chatting, Nell gaining in confidence as she explained the workings of her scheme. He didn't need to know that it had taken all her courage just to return to Venice with Molly. That just made it all the more important that she didn't return home empty-handed. He was right: dinner had been a good idea. She would do whatever it took to convince him the scheme would work—within reason, of course.

Reason played no part in Luca's thinking. He was working on blind instinct, feeling his way beneath Nell's defences any way he could, waiting for her to open up to him, needing that to happen before he could take things further. He wanted the inside track on what her plans were, and he wanted her...now more than ever.

CHAPTER SIX

TO GAIN her confidence Luca found himself telling Nell about the history of the *osteria* where they were eating dinner and his connection to it.

'My great-grandfather opened the restaurant at the end of the nineteenth century. It was called *Ai Tosi* then, "the boy's place" in Venetian dialect.' He returned Nell's look. 'Named after his two sons, Rico and Giuseppe, rather than for any other reason you might suppose.'

Her lips curved. Encouraged, he continued, 'The wine we're drinking now used to be brought by horse-drawn barge from the countryside around Venice, and then transported across the lagoon in rowing boats.'

Resting her chin on the heel of her hand, she stared at him, but jerked upright when he leaned across the table to refill her glass. His senses roared into overdrive. The fact that she was so aware of him was a timely reminder of the most demanding reason for his wanting this meeting.

'I don't think I ought to drink any more.' She placed her hand over the top of the glass.

'No pressure. Just leave it.'

'If you don't mind, I will.'

'But you should taste the sweet wine they bring with pudding. It's served with hot chestnuts. A speciality of the house, unmissable.'

'You make it sound irresistible.'

'It is.'

'You're spoiling me.'

Not half as much as he would like to! 'Nothing special—this is my local.'

'Your local?' Tipping her head to one side, Nell gave him a wry glance. 'I'd like to know where you go for a treat. Go on,' she encouraged. 'Tell me some more about this place.'

'Well, as I said, the sweet wine is a speciality of the house. It's the same wine my great-grandfather used to make when he was in charge here. You must try some, and eat the roasted chestnuts while you drink it.'

Irresistible, Nell thought again, which was as far as her thought processes could stretch before Luca went on and she was bewitched by the sound of his voice again.

'The cellar was equipped with large barrels, some of them weighing as much as five thousand kilograms, and others around seven hundred kilograms…'

His accent was like honey, soothing her senses, making her relax. She could have listened to him talking all night.

'The barrels had to be filled many times each year because the restaurant was so successful. But for the sweet wine…'

'Yes?' Nell found herself gazing, entranced, into Luca's eyes, and quickly straightened up. *Whirlwind romance… Love at first sight…* Random thoughts kept breaking into her concentration. But she was sensible, level-headed—more than that, she was on a mission. She couldn't afford to let daydreams take over.

But still…

'My great-grandfather kept his own equipment here on the premises to make it himself,' Luca was explaining. 'He crushed the grapes, and supervised the preparation of what soon became the most famous liquor in the region. And here it is.'

Along with the roasted chestnuts, it was just as delicious as Luca had promised. In fact, everything was perfect—apart from the fact that she hadn't got any sort of commitment to the pilot scheme from him. Perhaps over coffee…

'No,' Luca said when she suggested there was time for one small espresso. 'Let's not drink coffee here.'

'No?' Nell asked as he called for the bill. 'So where are we going to have coffee?' Not at his place, that was for sure!

'We'll take it with us.'

His eyes were warm, his reserved, courteous manner everything she could have hoped for. It reassured her. 'Take it with us? Where?' Suddenly she was buzzing with anticipation.

'It isn't every day you come to Venice, and I want to make this evening special for you.'

'Special how?'

'Just special.' Luca's smile died and his face turned serious suddenly. 'I shouldn't have said that as if you were a regular tourist. I haven't forgotten the last time you were here, Nell.'

'I didn't think you had.' As he reached out to touch her hand Nell felt Luca's confession had brought them another step closer.

'Good.' He exhaled and relaxed. 'You can't have many happy memories of Venice to look back on.'

'How could I?'

'Will you let me change that?'

There was nothing in his eyes but concern…concern, warmth, and maybe perhaps there was something more, but she didn't want to dwell on it in case she was mistaken. She settled on business instead. 'I would like an opportunity to tell you a bit more about what my organisation can bring to your hospital. We haven't done too much talking about business tonight, have we?'

'There's still time. Over coffee. If you'll come with me.'

'Oh…well…' She was wavering suddenly. Perhaps this wasn't a good idea. Surely the morning would do just as well. But did she really want the evening to end?

'Don't look so worried. I promise to give you a hearing.' He glanced at her. 'Now would be the best time, as I'm pretty tied up for the next couple of days.'

'Oh, well, then…'

The waiter distracted them, arriving with the bill and a flask of coffee. Nell smiled. 'I thought you were joking about taking it with us.'

'I never joke about coffee.'

Luca's eyes were full of humour, which Nell thought almost more dangerous than the wine. But still she said yes.

'We won't be going in a gondola, will we?' Irrational maybe, but the fear had never left her.

'Not a gondola,' Luca confirmed as they walked past a row of the traditional boats. He came to a halt beside a sleek white craft.

'I'm impressed.' Nell stared at it.

'Don't be. Practically everyone in Venice has a boat.' Luca dismissed the fabulous launch with a wave of his hand.

But not like this one, Nell guessed as he handed her on board.

'So, where are you taking me?' She acted cool, but she hadn't expected him to start casting off. An evening on board a fabulous yacht, alone with a man she found intensely attractive? She wasn't normally so reckless, but on this occasion—

'Out onto the lagoon,' Luca said, breaking into her thoughts. 'It's a sight everyone should see at least once in a lifetime. It's so magical at night—and it's a crucial part of my programme to rebuild your faith in Venice.'

'You don't need to go to all this trouble for my sake.'

'I want to.' He held her gaze for a moment. 'And it's my pleasure. I'm very proud of my city.'

With one last glance at the shore, Nell told herself not to be so silly. Luca wasn't going to try and seduce her on his boat. Anyway, it was her best chance to talk to him about her scheme without distraction.

Though surely she could have one night off, she thought rebelliously. A trip by moonlight along the shores of the most beautiful city in the world? How could she resist? Luca was right: this was a once-in-a-lifetime opportunity, and one she had no intention of squandering.

The black velvet sky was littered with stars, and the ancient buildings lining the San Marco Basin might have been made out of spun sugar with their dainty trelliswork picked out by moonlight. As Nell settled back on the comfortable leather seat her spine tingled at the thought that she would soon be gliding across the water, admiring the same sights that people for centuries had loved. And Luca hadn't been exaggerating when he said it would be beautiful. It was absolutely stunning.

'This is incredible.'

'Didn't I tell you? I'm going to drop anchor here and then we can have our coffee.'

'Do you come here often?' she teased.

'Only when I've got a really difficult case on my hands.'

'Are you suggesting I'm difficult, Doctor?'

'Difficult?' He gave a short laugh. 'You're one of the most complicated cases I've ever encountered.'

What was she doing? This was getting dangerous. She shouldn't be flirting with Luca, she should be talking about work. But her pulse disagreed. It had started racing the moment Luca had stopped the boat. How was she supposed to concentrate on work when he had brought her to one of the most romantic places in the world; when they'd had such a wonderful evening together, and that evening still had time to run? And when the biggest surprise of all had turned out to be the fact that they got on so well?

The truth was, deep down, she wanted to believe in romance again. To dare to love again, even. A secret affair in the most beautiful city on earth…

When Luca ducked his head inside the cabin to find coffee-cups for them Nell couldn't help noticing how lithe he was, how powerful. There was surely no harm in observing that much about him!

'Did the waiter know what you had planned tonight?' she asked when he emerged.

'I don't confide all my secrets in him.'

His expression was drawing her in, tempting her to believe everything she wanted to believe. One ebony brow arcing above sparkling eyes was all it took to make Nell wonder how many of Luca's secrets involved her. 'So you don't make a habit of this?'

'Do you care?'

Yes, she did—very much indeed. 'No, of course not,' she said flippantly.

He gave her a cup to hold and poured out the coffee. Clinking his tiny demi-tasse against hers, he murmured, 'To us.'

'To our successful association.'

'There's still a lot I need to know about this scheme of yours before I give the go-ahead.'

'I'll answer any question you care to ask.'

'Will you indeed?'

'Yes…' She hadn't missed the innuendo, and she hadn't meant to hold his gaze. Luca's smile was faint, but very dangerous.

And he was right: this was a magical place. That had to be the reason why things happened when they weren't supposed to, and why she was weakening at the very moment when she had to be strong. Silent messages were flying between them, insistent messages too powerful for her to resist…

Removing the coffee-cup from her hand, Luca leaned inside the cabin and stowed it with his own. Coming back, he smoothed a lock of hair that had fallen over her face. 'I like your hair longer. It suits you.' He tucked another wayward strand behind her ear.

A spasm of nerves hit Nell the moment Luca's fingers touched her face, but when he left her side to attend to something on the boat she wondered if she had got it wrong. She ached with longing, already missing him, missing his closeness, his attention. But when he came back he was cool, as if nothing special had happened between them.

And then his hand brushed hers lightly. Was that an accident? Did he mean something by it, or was she guilty of imposing her own desires on Luca's innocent actions? Her hand was still tingling while Luca seemed content to gaze out across the lagoon. Every part of her was tingling with awareness of how close he was, how alone they were…all the possibilities.

As the silence enveloped them Nell closed her eyes and inhaled deeply. The air was warm and softly fragranced with his scent, with hers and with the unmistakable salty smell of Venice. The only sound she could hear was gently lapping water and their mingled breathing: steady, regular, soothing. And then she felt Luca's fingers on the back of her neck, brushing her hair aside, tracing her earlobe…the lightest touch, feathering, then pulling away. Had she imagined that? Opening her eyes, she stared at him but he was gazing towards the opposite shore.

Leaning back against the rail, Nell turned her face up to the sky. Silence closed around them. And then she felt his warm hand touching her thigh. Was she imagining that too? Closing her eyes, she savoured the trail of fire he left behind him as he pushed up her skirt, stroking, searching, finding…

She didn't dare to breathe or move in case he stopped. Reckless or not, she needed him.

The back of his hand brushed between her legs, quickly, lightly, a frustrating butterfly's wing of a touch. But that was all it took for him to prove how swollen she was, how moist, how hot for him.

Exhaling on a sigh, Nell edged her legs apart, wanting so much more. But instead of giving her what she craved, Luca lifted his hand away. Somehow she stopped herself crying out with frustration, then gasped instead when he claimed her arms with a perfect blend of possession and reassurance. She couldn't pull away now, even had she wanted to. Tipping up her chin, she met his gaze. She wanted him and she wanted him to know it. Sweet fingers of arousal were caressing her body in the most delicious torture she had ever known: the strength in his hands, the curve of his lips, the delicious suspension of time he had created—she didn't want any of it to end.

'Must you wear this armour now?' Murmuring against her lips, he pushed the jacket from her shoulders.

Luca didn't know how close he had come to the truth, Nell thought as the jacket fell to the deck. It was her armour, and he was right: there was no need for it now.

Luca started on the buttons of her shirt, taking his time. He had to force himself to hold back or he knew he might be too rough with her. But it was taking every ounce of his willpower to slow the pace. When he let her shirt drop to the deck he sucked in his breath at the sight of the cobweb chemise she wore beneath. The thought of more delicate wrappings to remove excited him beyond belief. But it pleased him to take his time, because it pleased her, and he liked to see how aroused the delay made her.

Rolling her head back, she sighed, offering him the tender hollow at the base of her neck. Dipping his tongue, he licked and felt her tremble. Moving away again, he eased the delicate top over her head and let it flutter to the deck. The fastenings on her skirt were easily released and she had already slipped off her shoes when she climbed on board in deference to his teak decks.

She was wearing hold-ups beneath her skirt. Just who was torturing whom here? And how much more torture was he supposed to take?

Luca answered his own question silently: quite a lot more. The lacy tops clung to her firm, full thighs, leaving a tantalising hand-span of soft ivory flesh between that and the briefs she wore. They were so fine as to be almost transparent, and there was no mistaking how aroused she was.

The moment he captured her breasts would live with him forever. The pebbled nipples sent delight coursing through his overly sensitive finger pads. They appeared to be forcing themselves insistently through the flimsy fabric of her bra, and when he caressed them, lavishing them with the attention they deserved, he heard her whimper and the fire inside him raged into an inferno.

He removed the bra quickly, tossing it aside. The heaviness of her breasts was a revelation to him. He chafed her nipples again, more fiercely this time, relishing her cries of encouragement. Each new sound she made was a discovery that only intensified his pleasure. His senses were flooded with erotic heat. The scent of her hair, the warmth of her skin, the look on her face—all of it seemed designed to urge him on.

Luca knew just how much pressure to use, how to stroke and when to apply the firm touch she craved. She was melting into him, her body warm, moist, and swollen with desire. He lavished attention on her breasts until each taut nipple strained towards him. Her breasts had never looked so beautiful, Nell thought, as they did now in the dappled moonlight, nor had they ever felt so cherished and warm beneath a man's touch...

She cried out when Luca moved away, but before she had time to miss him he encircled her waist and dragged her close, dipping his fingers beneath the waistband of her briefs. Removing them in one easy movement, he swung her up, settling her onto a wooden platform. Nudging her thighs apart, he moved in close. His fingers found her wet, but evidently not wet enough, not as wet as Luca wanted her. And so he started stroking delicately, persuasively, responding intuitively to each sound she made. Resting her head against his chest, Nell relaxed completely, happily giving way to pleasure.

Hearing foil rip, she felt a brief surge of panic. He stopped immediately, even before she pressed her hands against his chest.

'Why?' he murmured against her mouth. 'Do you want me to stop?'

By then the moment of doubt had passed. She shook her head vigorously, and he began teasing her again, brushing her lightly before pulling away, until it was she who wrapped her legs around his waist to draw him close.

As his hands moved to cup her buttocks she spread her legs wide, leaning back within the secure curve of his arm and tilting up her hips to meet him. 'I need you now, Luca. Please, don't tease me any more. I need you to make love to me...'

She felt him tense briefly, but then he moaned as if the same spear of desire had pierced him too. Their free will was lost in that instant; they were both slaves to the same hunger, both willing captives. She couldn't think now; she could only feel as he filled her, stretching her beyond imagination, burying himself to the hilt, groaning with ecstasy as she closed her muscles around him to take him deeper. He didn't settle, or pause; she wouldn't let him. She asked and he gave, thrusting firmly, deeply, rhythmically rocking in time to her hungry cries, his body overwhelmed by the same force that gripped her. The waves of sensation built quickly for both of them and soon their wild cries were pealing out across the empty water.

That was just the start. Luca knew how to keep the pulse soft and low until she had recovered, when he increased the beat in time with her need. Having eaten, she wanted more, and soon she was feeding ravenously on pleasure again, luxuriating in his strength, in his virility. Luca was everything she had ever dreamed a man should be and never was, unselfish, intuitive…

As they came down from the peak together, Nell could see that Luca was as stunned as she by what had happened between them. For that brief time they had been free, and it was an abandon she found both exhilarating and terrifying, but it was a luxury she knew she would have no trouble getting used to.

Sex with Nell was a revelation for him. The intensity beyond belief, the pleasure unimaginable. It was as if the years of waiting, of thinking about her, had coalesced into this one fervid episode, and all the yearning in his heart had burst free. He wanted more of her than he had supposed. He wanted everything. He wanted all of her—

All of her body.

He had to be sensible, after all. They lived in different countries, led separate lives. It was extraordinary sex, but that was all it was. He needed to get real, and enjoy what they had while it lasted.

Luca carried her into the cabin, where they made love again to a more relaxed pace as they fell in with the gently rolling rhythms of the boat. Another ghost laid, Nell reflected as they lay quietly afterwards. After Jake's death it had crossed her mind that she might have failed him in bed and that was what had driven him into the arms of another woman…but if Luca was dissatisfied, he had a strange way of showing it.

'What are you looking so happy about?' There was a glint in his dark eyes as he caught her staring at him and rolled on top of her once more.

'This,' Nell whispered, taking him deep.

She felt so safe in Luca's boat. It was an erotic cocoon, a tiny dot on the vast lagoon—and that was also a metaphor of their night together. This encounter was a tiny dot on the vast map of their lives and wanting any more was foolish. But as the hours sped by, Nell discovered that even the past couldn't stop her wanting things she couldn't have.

It was approaching dawn when Luca sat up abruptly next to Nell's sleeping body.

What was he doing? Where was he going with this?

He'd wanted sex and he'd got what he wanted. That should be enough for him. But in the restaurant he'd enjoyed her company too—really enjoyed it. And sex with Nell had only left him wanting more.

But that wasn't practical, or realistic. He needed distance, thinking space. He didn't need to get involved, and she was clearly the kind of woman who got involved.

He had to make the break now before things got too complicated.

By the time he had buried his head in his hands and reflected for a few seconds, Luca had convinced himself that seducing Nell had been a mistake. It was up to him to nip it in the bud and make sure it didn't turn into a full-blown disaster—for both of them.

'Luca, what's wrong?' Nell awoke as he pulled away from

her to sit up, and felt the loss of him like a wound. He was resting his elbows on his knees, and his face was hidden from her.

'We should be going. I have to get up early.'

His voice was cool, dispassionate, and she felt snubbed. But then, hadn't he said he would be tied up for the next couple of days?

Yes, and wasn't that the reason she was supposed to have used this time to tell him about her scheme?

As Luca's words echoed in her head a cold hand tracked down Nell's spine. There had been something, something essential, missing from his voice. The tone that had been so teasing and warm before had turned detached, as if he were talking to a stranger. He hadn't used the voice of a man who had just been making love to a woman. He had spoken to her like one polite stranger to another.

'You can wash there.' He gestured abruptly towards the shower cabinet on board.

'Don't worry, I'll shower at the hotel,' she said. Suddenly she couldn't wait to get away. 'I won't keep you.'

If Luca had noticed the dig he didn't show it as he dressed. He kept his back turned to her, as if he wanted to shut her out. Nell kept telling herself that any moment he would turn to reassure her and draw her into his arms. They had shared so much; they had shared everything. Hadn't they?

With the last button on his shirt secured, Luca stood up and stretched. Easing past her, he ducked out of the cabin and went to raise the anchor with an electric winch. He took his seat at the bridge, switched on the engine and engaged the control lever, all without a word.

As the boat started moving towards the shore Nell remained where she was, sitting tensely on the edge of the bunk where they had made love. She didn't move again until Luca brought the boat alongside the landing stage at her hotel.

Her insides were ice as she stood up, but her face was flaming with humiliation. As she went to move past him he held out his hand to steady her as she stepped onto the shore. 'Thank you…' She stopped. What was she supposed to add? Thank you for a lovely evening? Taking a steadying breath, she fell back on, 'Thank you. That was a delicious meal.'

'I'm glad you enjoyed it,' he said without a trace of irony. 'See you at the meeting.'

She barely heard him, and only belatedly realised he had been saying something about a meeting. 'What time…?' But he had already turned the boat away and her voice was lost on the wind.

CHAPTER SEVEN

WHY had she trusted Luca enough to go to bed with him? Why had she stayed? Maybe because it was too easy to become complacent when you were safe in someone's arms, Nell reflected, careful not to let her feelings show. 'Has anyone called for me this morning, Marianna?'

'No one.'

'Are you sure?' Nell glanced at her wrist-watch. It was almost eleven o'clock.

'Of course she's sure, Mum. Why?'

As Molly's intelligent gaze searched her face, Nell turned away, afraid of what Molly might see. The cold ball of humiliation inside her was growing more indigestible every minute. 'No reason. I'm just waiting for feedback from last night.'

'From your dinner with Luca?'

'From my meeting with Luca.' Nell hated the betraying edge that always crept into her voice when she was lying. She didn't want to talk about Luca with guilt still pulsing through her veins. She had allowed herself to be a cheap one-night stand, which should never have happened. She should have remembered that he had walked out of her life once before. What had she been thinking?

She hadn't been thinking, of course. The carnal urge to

mate had been too strong. Playing so far out of her league meant wising up, or leaving casual sex to those who knew how to handle it.

Feeling two pairs of eyes trained on her face, Nell stared intently into her coffee-cup. She wasn't about to admit that she had already rung the hospital, having locked herself in the bathroom to make the call. Signor Barbaro couldn't be found, the man at the other end of the line had told her. Perhaps Signor Barbaro didn't *want* to be found—at least not by her.

Feeling Molly's gaze burning into her face, she tried to lighten the mood. 'So, what would you like to do today, Molly?'

'Dunno.'

Great! Her mood was catching. Nell turned to Marianna, but before she could speak the phone rang. They all tensed. After a moment Marianna went to answer it.

'Luca Barbaro for you,' she mouthed.

'Thank you.' Retreating into a corner of the room, Nell turned her back for some privacy. 'Hello?'

'Didn't we have an appointment this morning?' Luca sounded as if he had a thousand other things on his mind.

'You said you were tied up for the next couple of days, and I thought—'

'My schedule's unpredictable. You should have checked before deciding not to turn up.'

And you might have waited before turning your boat around to be sure I had heard! 'I apologise if I've kept you waiting. It seems I misunderstood.' Hurt was bubbling away inside her, but she couldn't forget why she was in Venice and the part Luca must play if the scheme was to be a success.

'Half an hour?' His tone was brisk.

'Yes, I'll be there.'

'They're expecting you at the gate. Collect a badge and come straight up.'

It was hardly the call she had been hoping for. Nell's expression hardened as she pictured Luca's arrogant face. How gracious of him to grant her an audience. Was this payment for services rendered? Did he think she used her body like an incentive-packed goodie bag?

But she had to calm down. Her pride had to take second place to the scheme—and like it or not, Luca Barbaro was the man she had to convince to establish her scheme in Venice, unless they were to completely redraw the plans they'd made.

It was time to put on her armour again.

Luca hadn't kissed her once, Nell realised as she sat down across from him. It hadn't occurred to her before, but now it did.

And wasn't that how people behaved when sex was an end in itself and the people involved meant nothing to each other?

And hadn't she walked into the situation with her eyes wide open?

Trust? There was no such thing between a man and a woman, Nell thought, opening up her briefcase. Bringing out the documents she had prepared for Luca, she made a silent vow not to leave until she had his co-operation.

'Would you like a glass of water?'

Did she look pale? She didn't want him suspecting how she felt inside. 'For some reason I'm feeling the heat today. I'll be fine in a moment.'

'I'll get you a glass of water anyway and turn up the air-conditioning.' Leaving his seat, he walked across the room.

Even now she couldn't look at him without trembling—and it was impossible not to look at him. Did she want to see how beautifully coordinated he was, how perfectly balanced?

Dragging her gaze away, Nell forced her mind back to the business at hand. 'Would you like to look at these?' She pushed some papers across the desk. 'I thought they'd give you some idea of what we do.'

'I'd rather hear it from you than read some glossy brochure prepared by your marketing people.' Putting the glass of water down in front of her, Luca returned to his seat.

'Marketing people?' Nell held his gaze. 'Ours is a small volunteer-based scheme. I don't use marketing people. I wrote every word on these pages myself.'

'Still…' Leaning back, he rested his head on his arms. 'I'd like you to tell me about it.'

And she'd thought she had put every safeguard in place. How could she remain immune to him? He was such a powerful masculine force, he was impossible to ignore. But did he even remember last night? Or were there so many similar nights for Luca Barbaro, he barely marked their passing? If so, she hoped he remembered to change the sheets…

'Would you like to begin?'

Corralling her wandering thoughts, Nell launched straight in.

'So we're to be the guinea pigs for your pilot scheme?' Luca interrupted after she had been talking for a few minutes.

'I thought you might be happier testing my assertions for yourself. How about Monday for a tour of the hospital and a trial run? What do you think?' she pressed when he didn't reply.

What did he think? He had to be impressed by the way she was handling a difficult situation. He was tempted to let her try the pilot scheme. And the itch he had scratched last night had started up again. 'What do I think?' He rasped a thumb across the stubble on his chin and held her gaze. It pleased him to see her eyes darken, but beneath the front he sensed she was wary. He wanted her again. If nothing else the pilot scheme she had suggested would throw them together.

And between now and Monday? He couldn't concentrate

on work while his mind was full of Nell. And his mind was
firmly lodged beneath his belt. A little to one side of that was
a pocket full of supplies.

'I think…'

'Yes?' She became instantly alert.

'I think I need to know a lot more about you before I agree
to this pilot scheme.'

'More about me?' Nell shook her head, suddenly incensed.
What more did he need to know? After last night she could
only conclude that giving every appearance of enjoying someone's company was an act as far as Luca was concerned—an
act for which he expected payment in kind. 'I've told you all
you need to know about me. The project is what's important.'

As Nell swallowed, it drew Luca's attention to the pulse
fluttering at the base of her throat, and lust roared up inside
him. There was a red mist dancing in front of his eyes that
had no bearing on her project, but as a whipping boy it served
him well. 'So, I'm to allow you, a woman I hardly know, into
my hospital with your band of volunteers, trained who knows
how, just on your say-so?'

'Not on my say-so. On my track record, and on all those
recommendations from other establishments I have brought
here for you to study.'

'That will take time, and then I'll have more questions.'

'I'll give you all the time you need.'

Perfect. He curbed his smile as he dipped his head in acknowledgement of the offer. He could see she was gritting her
teeth, while he was trying to calm the lustful little demon lashing
about inside him. He wanted sex…sex with no hang-ups, no
consequences, no complications. But life was never that simple.

What was going through Luca's mind? Nell was still stinging
with humiliation from last night—and what was worse, she

still wanted him. But whatever had happened last night, she had to take the project forward. She wasn't going anywhere until she got his agreement to host the pilot scheme. It had become a matter of pride now.

The shutters were drawn, his eyes were dark and the air was sultry. Exactly how far *was* she prepared to go to ensure that he didn't back out of the scheme?

She shook away the thought. But it was one thing making angry resolutions at a safe distance, quite another keeping them when she was shut in a small room with Luca. How could she not be aware of him when she was still throbbing from his extremely thorough attentions? Responding to the thought, Nell eased her position on the seat.

'Getting hot, Nell?' Luca murmured, sending another fire-ball of arousal flooding through her.

'No, I'm fine. Your air-conditioning is very efficient.'

He only had to raise a brow to call her a liar.

The tension in the air was growing harder to ignore by the minute. She started telling him about the project to channel her thoughts in a safe direction, but she was fully aroused, which made her thoughts disjointed, and she could see Luca was only paying lip-service to what she was saying. She couldn't blame him. She was hardly making sense.

As she handed some documents across the desk, thinking it would keep him busy while she pulled herself together, their hands touched. The moment hung in the air, connecting them by a stream of tension that had to find release.

They came together like a raging tornado, Luca's post-coital brush-off consumed in the heat along with all Nell's other complaints against him. He could satiate her most basic need, and that was all she cared about. His arms were so welcome, strong and familiar, and the scent of him was in-toxicating as he dragged her close. He backed her towards the door and she heard the key turn in the lock, and as he swung her up she cried out, already anticipating pleasure. There were no preliminaries. Luca just wedged her against the wall and dragged up her skirt. At the same time he was pulling down her briefs, he was unfastening his zip. And the next moment he was sinking inside her, holding her safe, fastening her legs around his waist, his hands firm on her buttocks. Spreading her wide, he pounded hard, fast.

'You want this, don't you, Nell?'

'Yes… Oh, yes!' Pleasure so wild, so intense it made their previous encounter seem tame? She wanted it.

'Tell me,' he instructed her fiercely. 'Tell me everything you want from me. I have to hear you say it.'

Words poured from her lips, words she didn't recognise, harsh, crude words that brought a look of brutal satisfaction to Luca's face. 'I want you, Luca. I want more!'

'Like this?' he suggested.

'Oh, *yes*…' She gasped as he rolled from side to side and the pleasure mounted.

'And this?'

How could she answer while Luca was talking roughly in her ear, telling her in Italian, in English what she wanted, what she needed, and what he was going to give her? Nell's mouth fell open 'Yes, yes…' She groaned and dug her fingers into him, bucking convulsively as he took her to a level of pleasure she had never experienced before. All thoughts of holding back, or preserving some propriety were lost in the urge to offer herself for his attentions, to angle her body, to part her legs wider still, to use her hands now to open herself more for him. And Luca responded intuitively, keeping the pleasure building until Nell reached a peak so high she was frightened to fall off it…

'Now,' he ordered fiercely, thrusting fast and deep.

With a cry she rushed over the edge, grinding her hips greedily against him. He made it last for the longest time, serving her selflessly, skilfully, while she gasped and shrieked with pleasure like some wild creature that recognised no boundaries.

At last the explosion softened into a series of delicious aftershocks, and after soothing her Luca took his turn, building the rhythm again until he found savage release in a series of powerful thrusts that incredibly brought Nell to the brink again so that this time they plunged into the abyss together.

Lowering her gently to her feet, Luca was careful to steady her, but then he stood back and she heard him fasten his fly as he crossed the room.

'There are some tissues on the desk.'

His voice was calm, impersonal. And why not? His job was done. As she slipped on her briefs, she had to wonder about her sanity. She had to wonder about a man whose heart was nothing more than a pump, with about as much feeling as one of his hospital machines. She had let lust get the better of her again, and now she was going to pay the price. If only she'd thought things through first, this would never have happened. But she hadn't thought at all—she'd had one goal in mind, and she'd reached that rather faster than she had expected.

It wasn't until she had finished dressing and had bent down to slip on her sandals that Nell noticed the discarded foil.

He had come prepared. He had been expecting this.

Rage exploded out of her. 'You cold-hearted bastard!'

'What?' Turning, Luca levelled a quizzical stare on her face. 'What's wrong with you?'

'What's wrong with me?' Picking up the packet from the floor, Nell threw it at him. 'Do you keep a store of these in your office, just in case?' She firmed her lips when he didn't answer. 'You had this planned all along, didn't you, Luca? I can't believe I've been taken in again!'

'You're a grown woman. You knew what you were doing. Would you rather I had taken no precautions at all?'

'Of course not—'

'Then why are you complaining?'

He was so cool she could hardly speak. But as he turned she grabbed his arm. Before she knew what she was doing, she had raised her hand to him.

Catching hold of her wrist, Luca dragged her close and kissed her hard. She fought him off, but he knew her too well, and in a moment she was kissing him back—hungrily, desperately.

Luca pulled away first, holding her at arm's length to give her a long, lazy smile. That smile, Nell realised, told her the kiss was just more proof of his domination.

Shaking as she wiped the back of her hand across her mouth, she held his gaze. 'Why am I complaining? I'm surprised you need to ask.'

Luca's lips pressed down as he eased his shoulders in a shrug. 'You seemed like a willing partner to me.'

'But there has to be more to sex than—'

'Than what, Nell?' Grabbing her arms, he drew her close to stare into her eyes, and then abruptly he let her go again. There was too much in her eyes…things he didn't want to see.

She lashed out at him again, this time with words. 'Do you know how much I hate you? You make me feel dirty!'

Dirty? Reeling back, he realised she couldn't have said anything to shock him more. Yes, their relationship was like nothing he had ever known before—casual but intense, disturbing…and dirty? His blinding flash of shame turned to anger. She had struck at the core of his self-belief. He was a principled man, a man who kept a fence around him for a reason. How could he do his work without denial, without self-restraint? His life was ruled by objectivity; there was no room in it for personal considerations. His emotional austerity had never been breached before, and it couldn't be breached in the space of a few days by a woman he hardly knew.

'Dirty? What are you talking about?'

'How do you describe having sex up against a wall?'

There wasn't much he could say to that. He watched her straighten her clothes, sensing she was straightening out her thoughts at the same time. Once she'd finished, she turned to face him. Her eyes had turned to blue ice.

'Nothing to say, Luca?'

'What do you want me to say?'

With a mirthless laugh she shook her head. 'I might have been a fool to fall for this again, but you are one cold, hard bastard.'

'What's your problem, Nell?'

'What's *my* problem? I'm not the one with a problem. You've got the problem, Luca. You don't know the meaning of emotion. You don't have a feeling, caring bone in your body!'

He was still stinging from her earlier attack. 'Isn't that an overreaction to what was some rather good sex?'

Nell shook her head. 'Your conceit overwhelms me.'

'Don't burden me with your emotional baggage. We had good sex, we both enjoyed it, end of story.'

Nell's face reflected her incredulity. 'You are something else…'

'I'm a man.'

'And a doctor,' she observed softly and ironically. 'What a perfect combination.'

'Meaning?'

'It explains your frame of mind.'

'You'll have to do better than that,' he snapped, angry at her and with himself for reacting to her nonsense.

'All right, I will. I never told you how my husband died, did I?'

Luca raised his brows. 'Does that have relevance?'

Shooting a glance at the ceiling, Nell gave a short, humourless laugh. 'Oh, yes, Luca, I think it does. Jake died because of medical incompetence. And after he died I was left waiting, not told anything, deliberately deceived, while other doctors scrambled to cover for their colleague's mistake. You wanted to know how I fund this project, how I got it off the ground? The hospital had to pay out for their doctor's mistake, that's how.'

'I still don't see—'

'No, you wouldn't. Just a tick here, and a cross there, and Jake's tragic accident was a cover-up in which his whole medical team was embroiled. They treated me like a piece of no-account dirt. They ignored me, patronised me, lied to me, fobbed me off with medical terminology and gobbledygook. I only found out the truth about what really happened at the inquest.'

'But what does this have to do with me?'

'It's a state of mind, Luca. Think back to when Molly was taken sick. Have you any idea how much worse you made that experience with your coldness, your impatience, your unpleasantness towards me? I was in despair. I was desperate. I thought my baby was going to die, like my husband had, and you just shut me out!'

'My concern was for the child—'

'*The child?* You've met Molly, you know her, and yet you can still only see her as the child, the patient, the statistic! What's *wrong* with you?'

'There's nothing wrong with me—and I hope you're not bracketing me with the incompetents who handled your husband's case!'

'Listen to you.' She raked her hair, and then looked at him

almost as if she felt sorry for him. 'Still hanging on to your pride. Jake's case, as you call it, was his life. My husband's life, Luca.'

'You have my condolences.'

'Your condolences?' There was a disbelieving laugh in Nell's voice. 'Patients are just so many records on a computer file as far as you're concerned. With no character or history to flesh out the individual. Is it just me, or is that how you treat all your sexual partners too?'

'No!' he cut across her. For a moment he was speechless; she had really shocked him. She had held a mirror up in front of his face and he didn't like what he saw. Was that how she saw him? Was that how he was? Was he guilty of treating both his patients and his partners like bodies to be processed for the best possible outcome?

Had he failed to treat Nell as a woman all those years ago on the canal—as a mother, as a fellow human being? And if so, what was his excuse? Oh, yes…he was a doctor.

It sounded pretty thin now. And yes, he had been busy, stressed-out, exhausted…but he had still been a human being, and he could have related to her on that level for however short a time. Instead he had presumed that she wouldn't understand, that he was too busy, that his knowledge was too specialised for a mere civilian to comprehend.

Or had he just been too self-important to consider her feelings? And was he still guilty of that now? It was too late to wish he'd done things differently all those years ago…was it too late for him to change?

It hardly mattered, Luca realised. His intention not to complicate things with Nell had backfired on him in the most spectacular fashion. It might have taught him something, but if this was a new beginning for him, as far as Nell was concerned, it was the end.

'I'd like to confirm that my volunteers are still welcome here on Monday.'

Her voice was shaking, but her eyes told him she was as determined as ever. And he had been preparing to reap the whirlwind of her personal hurt. She had surprised him yet again.

'Monday?'

'Have you changed your mind?' She held his gaze.

He hesitated. 'How are we going to—?'

She cut him off. 'Going to what, Luca? Separate our work from what has happened between us? That's easy,' she said before he had a chance to answer. 'We won't spend any time together that isn't directly connected to the project. Unless of course you're going to allow your personal life to interfere with improvements to your hospital services?'

He felt as if he was standing on a rapidly shrinking ice floe, and hit back the only way he knew how. 'Don't be in any doubt, Nell. I always put the hospital first.'

'Good. Then I'll see you on Monday. You'll find I've put everything you need in this information pack for you. You can check all the references of the volunteers, and if there's anything you're unsure of, don't hesitate to get in touch.'

His admiration went up a notch. She'd been profoundly upset, and still remained true to her purpose. He was thankful for the project too—it was all they had left now. But still his natural caution stepped in.

'I make no promises. I'll read everything and then talk to a few people.'

'Procrastinate?'

'Make a considered judgement.'

They held each other's gaze. She was as stubborn as he was. He sensed this was a pivotal moment. 'So…Monday,' he said as casually as he could.

'Yes?'

'I'll tell the security guard to expect your people for the pilot scheme. We'll go ahead for now. There'll be badges waiting at the gate. I'm presuming you'll be with the group?' He couldn't believe her answer meant so much to him.

'Of course.'

Instead of allowing her triumph to show, she behaved professionally, coolly, as if this was the outcome she had expected all along. How she felt about the man making the offer was similarly buried. Silently, he saluted her.

Risk-taking was new to him, but it was apparent that there was no such thing as casual sex with Nell. He had to change something, or there would be no sex at all—and that wasn't something he was prepared to factor into his calculations.

'See you on Monday. If not before…'

Not before, Nell thought, allowing a slight smile of acknowledgement to touch her lips as she gathered up her things. She was still throbbing from sex, heated from their argument, reeling from Luca's unexpected agreement to take in her scheme. But more than all that, she was stunned by the way she had opened up to him. What kind of fool exposed so much of herself to a man who didn't know the meaning of emotion?

CHAPTER EIGHT

'YOU did what?' Nell blenched.

'I rang up Luca and invited him round for tea,' Molly repeated blithely.

'How on earth did you find his number?' Nell's mind was racing. After everything that had happened between them, all the pain that had spilled out of her, she just wanted to forget—to put some distance between them. She had started to do just that even before she left Luca's office. And now this!

'I rang the hospital, told them I was a former patient and asked to speak to him. They put me through. You don't mind, do you, Mum?'

What had happened between Luca and herself wasn't Molly's fault, Nell realised. Should she make a fuss and risk provoking curiosity even more, or just grit her teeth and go along with it? 'No, dear, I don't mind.'

No, dear? Out of the corner of her eye Nell saw Marianna's raised eyebrows. Was this what it had come to? Had raising the barricades against Luca made her into some sort of stuffy Victorian mama? 'Sorry!' Dropping to her knees, she held out her arms. 'Give me a hug, Moll, I need it. It's been one of those days.'

'I thought you saw Luca today?'

'I did!' Nell used a comic voice and pulled a face as if she had encountered a troll. To her relief Molly started laughing.

'But you don't mind if he comes to tea?'

'Too late to worry now.' And what could go wrong with Molly and Marianna around to back her up?

They arranged to eat outside on the balcony overlooking the Grand Canal. She would find an opportunity to draw him aside and tell him that this was the first and last time they would be meeting like this. Luca had been Molly's doctor and this was a nice way for Molly to thank him— but that was it.

Molly had made all the arrangements—ringing Room Service to place her order, and then Housekeeping to make sure they had enough cushions for an extra guest. She had even set the table by herself, arranging the floral centrepiece provided by the concierge and positioning candles either side of it.

'Candles in broad daylight? It isn't dark yet,' Nell pointed out.

'Don't be so boring, Mum. Remember, this is Venice. It's supposed to be romantic.'

'Romantic?'

'A romantic city, I mean,' Molly quickly amended.

And then Nell was too busy pacing up and down trying to convince herself she could handle tea with Luca to notice what was going on. It was only when the knock came on the door and Marianna and Molly got there before her that she realised they were both dressed to go out.

'Where do you think you two are going?'

'Out.' Molly tipped her chin as she stared at her mother.

'But you can't go out! What about tea?' For a moment, Nell thought Molly might relent. It was a proper English afternoon tea, their favourite: scones, jam and cream, breakfast tea with either milk or lemon, and soft sponge cakes coated in chocolate and toffee sauce to eat afterwards.

Molly stared at the tray longingly. 'Sorry—things to do, people to see. Isn't that right, Marianna?'

Marianna had perfected the art of staring off into the middle distance, Nell thought, glaring at her.

'Don't look so worried, Mum! It'll be fun!'

Fun? What had Luca been thinking, accepting Molly's invitation? 'You're probably right.' She didn't want to get into an argument.

The buzzer went.

'Luca.' As Nell opened the door, she hoped her eyes said what her voice couldn't in front of Molly and Marianna—that he should have found an excuse not to come.

A bemused expression crossed his face as Molly and Marianna walked past him. 'I'm sorry. I thought…'

'Yes, so did I. Do you want to come in? You don't have to,' Nell assured him sincerely once they had turned the corner.

'Don't be silly.' He walked in knowing he had been conned, and by a ten-year-old. He'd never guessed women started so young. He felt some explanation was necessary. 'Nell…'

Shutting the door, she leaned back against the wall. 'Luca?'

The call from Molly had taken him by surprise, but afternoon tea had sounded so innocent he hadn't dreamed it was a set-up. He stared outside at the balcony, where deep-cushioned seats had been drawn up to a table draped in a damask cloth. For once he was lost for words and barely managed a lame, 'This is nice.'

'What are you doing here, Luca?' There were only two chairs, Nell noticed now, cursing her inattention to detail.

'Molly invited me. I assumed it was your idea…' Clearly not, he thought, seeing Nell's expression. 'Next time I speak to her, I'll—'

'There won't be a next time, Luca. There's no reason for you to contact Molly. I won't have her misled.'

'Misled?'

Isn't it blindingly obvious? She doesn't have a dad and she's considering you for the role. 'I won't have her misled into thinking you're a friend,' Nell clarified. 'I didn't want to raise her suspicions by saying no to this scheme of hers—before I knew she was planning to disappear—but *you* should have had the good sense not to come.'

'I didn't want to disappoint her.'

And now he'd developed feelings?

'I won't have Molly sensing how tense we are around each other. I don't want you here, Luca. I thought I made that clear yesterday. Anything we have to say to each other can be said in the workplace or on the telephone.'

He dipped his head in ironic acknowledgement, and she didn't move until he left the room. Even the way he shut the door, with a barely discernible click, seemed designed to mock her.

Eyes shut, Nell analysed her feelings. Her heart was pounding. She still wanted him. It was that simple.

She had to fight the urge to rush to the door to call him back. She waited until she was sure that he'd gone before letting out her breath in a juddering stream. Only then was her gaze drawn to the tray of dainty sandwiches and cakes waiting for them out on the balcony. Stalking across the room, she picked up the tray and tossed the contents into the canal.

She couldn't settle. She paced the room until Molly and Marianna returned from their walk.

'Did it go well?' Molly asked eagerly.

'As well as could be expected,' Nell said honestly. 'If you'd stayed you would have been able to help us eat the cakes.'

'You ate everything?' Molly gazed at the empty tray.

'Er, yes. Every scrap.' A white lie was necessary, Nell decided.

'But you didn't light the candles,' Molly observed.

'Shall we go out?' Nell changed the subject. The last thing

she wanted was to enter into a conversation about Luca, a man so divorced from normal human feelings she wouldn't have been surprised if he had been stamped *cold-hearted* end to end like a stick of rock.

As Nell had hoped, Molly's interest switched immediately. 'Where would we go?'

'I don't know...but I've decided that it's time you and I and Marianna had an adventure.'

Nell began to relax as the water taxi travelled across the lagoon. This was better than moping around at the hotel. There was no point in trying to protect Molly from believing Luca would remain part of their lives, and then spoiling it all by being miserable. She had made a mistake, but she could and she would get over him—and Molly deserved some fun.

Like many cities in warm climates, Venice came alive in the evening. This was their first trip to one of the smaller islands on the tidal flats. Nell had asked the concierge at the hotel for suggestions for their night out, and he had mentioned a celebration to commemorate the end of the sixteenth-century plague. It would be like one big party, he had told her, and Nell thought it sounded like a good experience for Molly. She had bought them all fearsome long-beaked masks, explaining to Molly that Venetians had once filled these with herbs and other sweet-smelling medicaments, which they believed kept them safe from the disease.

'You look gross,' Molly commented, when Nell put hers on.

'Well, perhaps we won't put them on until we get there.'

Molly wasn't listening. She was too busy peering out of the window at the other craft travelling in convoy with them across the lagoon. All the vessels were dressed with lanterns and greenery, and Nell could see that many of the passengers were in full costume. The women were wearing elaborate silk gowns in every colour of the rainbow, while the men wore close-fitting breeches with cloaks flung around their shoulders. It made them look like gallants of old escorting their beautiful masked companions to a romantic tryst.

The sense of anticipation increased as the fleet drew closer to the island. It was as if they were escaping back to another age, Nell thought. Seeing Molly's face pressed to the window, she smiled wryly. It was about time she made a good decision.

'Come on,' she said when they docked. 'We don't want to get left behind.' With Marianna on one side of Molly and Nell on the other, they hurried on shore to follow the crowd streaming along the dockside towards the shady alleyways leading to the town centre.

When they reached the main square it was packed. 'Stay close to me,' Nell warned Molly and Marianna, 'I don't want you to be swept away. There are so many people here. I had no idea it would be so busy.'

In the middle of the square was a large fountain. Around this were colourful stalls, and, lining the edge of the square, elegant houses set like jewels amongst tiny boutiques with leaded light windows. Flowers tumbled from wrought-iron balconies, splashing colour across ancient walls, and there were banners and flags hanging everywhere. Amongst the crowd, street entertainers on stilts with striped baggy trousers, painted faces and top hats appeared like fantastic creatures from another world. There were musicians playing—several bands at once, all of them competing for the crowd's attention. The noise was incredible, but Nell found it exhilarating. Biting her bottom lip, she turned full circle, hardly knowing which way to look first.

Then there was an explosion above, and everyone around her was staring into the sky, staring and pointing to the fireworks, which she presumed must mark the start of the celebrations. As cheers and laughter erupted all around them, she held on tight to Molly.

'I can't see,' Molly complained.

'I'll try and lift you up.' But it was difficult. There was such a press of people, and Nell had to be content with squeezing into a corner behind a food stall, where Molly could stand on a step between her and Marianna.

'Isn't it wonderful?' Molly cried excitedly clapping her hands.

'Yes, it is,' Nell shouted back. They couldn't have been any-where but Italy with the noise and exuberance, glitter and glamour. The craziness and abandon so perfectly reflected the soul of a people who wore their hearts on their sleeves and kept their faces turned to the sun. The mouth-watering scent of food teased their nostrils, and there was the heady fragrance of young wine, candle-wax, perfume, gunpowder... And now people were dancing, the couples swinging each other round to the energetic rhythms provided by a small group of elderly men dressed in traditional costume who were playing the har-monica, the accordion, the fiddle and the drum. Immediately a nearby group started up in competition, and then another and another. It was chaos, but such wonderful chaos.

Most people had taken the trouble to dress up like those she had seen on the boats, and nearly everyone was masked. It lent an air of mystery, of romance, a sense that anything was possible. Molly quickly put her mask on, though it kept slipping off, and Nell was sorry she hadn't noticed before now how big it was.

'I wish we'd come in proper costume.' Molly had to tug off her mask so that Nell could hear her above the noise.

Downing her own mask, Nell agreed.

'Perhaps if we come again next year?'

Nell was just about to put the damper on that idea when suddenly her eyes were covered from behind and she shrieked. Molly shrieked too—with excitement.

In that instant Nell knew who it was, though recognising him did nothing to stop her heart from pounding.

She turned to see a tall, powerfully built figure dressed from head to toe in black. The plain black mask enhanced his strong, saturnine features, and he wore a black cloak lined with scarlet silk. 'Luca?'

He made a bow. 'We are all anonymous here, lady.'

'But it is you!' Staring up, Molly clutched his hand.

'In Venice we wear masks so that everyone is equal, and even a humble man like me may offer his services to three beautiful ladies.' He acknowledged Marianna, and bowed to Nell, who gasped as he swung Molly onto his shoulders.

'Shall we go?' he invited.

Nell was so stunned by Luca's unexpected arrival she couldn't think of a single word to say. At least for Molly's sake he seemed prepared to overlook his frosty reception at the hotel. Perhaps it was better to keep it that way. 'Go where?' she said at last.

'Anywhere the music takes us.'

'Yes, let's!' Molly checked with Nell. 'Can we?'

With most of his face hidden behind the mask, Luca's lips appeared crueller and more sensuous than ever. The dark glint in his eyes warned Nell to be cautious. She couldn't forget his savage kiss, or their impassioned encounters. But she needed him—the project needed him—and she didn't want to cause a fuss in front of Molly. She had to balance her mistrust against her duty...

'Don't forget,' he said, 'we're all anonymous here.'

'Please, Mum!'

Molly was pressing her to make a decision. Ripping her away now would cause an ugly scene, leaving doubts, questions Nell couldn't, and didn't want to provide answers for. But just one night, one anonymous night behind masks... It didn't mean she had to start trusting him. She could let go, be herself. Or rather, be the person she longed to be...

Before Nell had chance to state her decision, a glamorous older woman came out of the crowd towards them.

'*Bellissima!* What a pretty child!'

She was wearing full costume like Luca, her face almost completely hidden behind an elaborately jewelled mask. 'Would you like me to take a picture of your group?' She pointed to the camera swinging from Nell's wrist.

Nell smiled politely. 'No, thank you.' The last thing she wanted was a reminder of Luca. But wasn't it rude and unreasonable of her to refuse the offer? 'I don't want to trouble you,' she amended.

'It's no trouble, I assure you. It will make a lovely souvenir for you to take home.'

The accent was so attractive. Nell guessed she was Italian, possibly even Venetian like Luca. She handed over the camera. 'Thank you. *Grazie,*' she added when the picture had been taken.

'*Prego,*' the woman said, smiling as she disappeared into the crowd.

'Now, come along, Molly,' Nell said firmly. 'I'm sure Signor Barbaro is here with friends. We mustn't keep him—'

'Signor Barbaro? Who is this Signor Barbaro?' Luca demanded, turning his head up to Molly. 'Do you know him?'

Molly threw herself happily into the conspiracy. 'No!'

'I can assure you, ladies, I am entirely at your service.'

'Just a minute!' Nell was forced to chase after them as Luca strode off through the crowd with Molly sitting on his shoulders. She caught up with him by the fountain and grabbed his arm. 'We're going back to the hotel now. It's well past Molly's bedtime—'

'But the main firework display is at midnight. Won't you be staying for that?'

'How can we? Once it's over all these people will want to go back to Venice. We'll never find a water taxi—'

'And so you'll come back on my boat—'

'Oh, *yes!*' Molly agreed enthusiastically.

'Absolutely not!' Nell's mouth tightened as she turned to glare at him.

'Why not?' Luca said.

A thousand reasons blazed from Nell's eyes as she stared at him, none of which she could give voice to while Molly was in earshot. 'Because we can't possibly impose on you?'

'It's no imposition. There are so many small canals criss-crossing our city; it is only a short distance from one side to the other by water.'

For a time they were silent, while the party carried on around them. Nell realised that if she wanted Molly to remain unaware of the currents between herself and Luca, refusing his offer of a lift home was unhelpful. This was what they were here for after all…an evening of fun.

Nell looked up, realising Luca was saying something. 'I'm sorry?'

'I was just explaining to Molly that they should have told you in the shop that this type of mask is generally worn by men. Will you allow me to make amends?'

Nell's heart turned over as Luca stared at her. She sensed his question went a lot deeper than the masks.

Molly distracted them both. 'I told you they were gross.'

'Well, I thought they would teach you something important about the history of Venice. The plague, and how it affected all of Europe—'

'Commendable, I'm sure,' their masked companion observed drily. 'But there are other more interesting, and possibly less ghoulish, tales about Venice that Molly might want to hear.'

'Like what?' Molly pressed, instantly grasping the fact that it might be possible to extend the conversation until the fireworks started.

'Harlequin and Columbine, for one.'

'*Please!*' Molly looked down at Nell again.

Tantrums she could deal with firmly, but when Molly was making a perfectly reasonable request, how was she supposed to refuse without seeming to be a killjoy?

'Well, perhaps we can stay long enough for you to hear about Harlequin and Columbine…'

It surprised Luca to discover how much he wanted to be part of their adventure. The sight of Nell with her daughter touched him. She had tried to bring the carnival alive for Molly, and if she hadn't quite pulled it off he wasn't going to leave her to flounder this time. 'And then long enough after for that for me to find new masks for the three of you?'

'We couldn't possibly accept,' Nell protested.

'Why not?' Molly stared first at her mother and then at him.

Luca found himself warming under the sense of responsibility. 'Why not?' he repeated gently, looking at Nell.

'Because…'

'I'd really like to—I'd like the chance to share our customs, our holiday with you. Won't you let me?'

'When you put it like that…'

There was a moment—no, more than a moment—when he felt a new and very different kind of triumph. But Molly was shrieking with excitement, and before he could identify what it meant he was forging a passage for their little group through the crowd and heading for the shops.

Which was how they came to be watching fireworks at midnight after a night of dancing and eating sweet, crispy pastries still warm from the oven. And then one of the bands struck up a tarantella, and Luca insisted they must all join in the dance.

'Not again! I can't,' Nell protested, but it was no use; Luca's enthusiasm was irrepressible, and it was such fun dancing with a crowd of Italian families. All age groups were represented, teenagers dancing unashamedly with their grandparents, mothers with their sons. Then a grey-haired gallant swept Marianna into the action. Nell couldn't resist now!

Laughter and shrieks were erupting all around them, and then Luca swung both Molly and Nell off their feet and whirled them round and round until they were dizzy. The moment the music finished in a crashing finale, he lifted Molly onto his shoulders again and went in search of some ice cream.

'I really can't!' Nell looked incredulously at the giant-sized cone he was holding out to her.

'Tonight you can,' their masked companion assured her. 'Tonight you must forget the usual and allow the fantastic to take you over. It is one of the first rules of carnival.'

They had barely finished the ice cream when Luca insisted they visit the sideshows. There were fortune-tellers, hoop-la, and a shooting gallery, where he excelled, and finally apple-bobbing, where Molly was surprised to find something that reminded her of home.

'Festivals are much the same the world over,' Luca explained. 'And where there are apples, there is apple-bobbing. Shall we make your mother take a turn?'

Nell tried until she was helpless with laughter, but she still couldn't manage to secure a single apple in the barrel of water.

'You need sharp teeth for this,' Luca advised, collecting one for her with a flourish.

Nell held his gaze a beat too long, and knew she was blushing by the time she looked away.

'I'm glad the masks don't stop you eating ice cream.'

'The masks make anything possible,' Luca assured Molly, who was now wearing the child-sized mask he'd bought her— a fabulous thing, extravagantly decorated with sequins and feathers. 'A humble man may dance with a noblewoman, a milkmaid with a prince—'

'Or a simple doctor with three grand ladies,' Nell suggested impishly, flourishing her own rather elegant mask, which was attached to the end of a white-painted stick. It was the Columbine mask Molly had insisted she choose. Nell had been relieved when Luca could not be persuaded to exchange his plain black mask for a matching Harlequin, quartered in the same red, black, white and bronze.

'But they make a pair,' Molly had protested.

Exactly, Nell's eyes had seemed to say as she stared at Luca, so don't you dare buy that mask!

'I think I'll leave it,' he had said, shooting an ironic glance at Nell—and the plague masks were tactfully left behind in the shop.

But after the apple-bobbing Molly started to flag. 'We'd better get back now,' Nell said. 'You don't have to leave, Luca, we can get a water taxi.' She could see that none of the Italians were ready for home yet, and so it was a good time to leave. There were plenty of small craft lined up at the edge of the canal, waiting to take passengers back to the city.

'Why don't I take Molly back?' Marianna suggested. 'There's no reason why you should have to leave, Nell. I'm perfectly capable of taking her home. In fact I'm a little tired myself,' she added, smothering a yawn. 'So, if you don't mind…'

It was hard for Nell to disagree. 'Of course I don't mind.'

'And I'll find you a taxi—make sure it's someone I know, who will look after you,' Luca offered.

Striding to the landing stage, he called a man over and Nell saw that money was changing hands. 'You didn't need to do that,' she insisted when he returned. 'I would have paid—'

'Older customs prevail during carnival. One such tradition demands that a man must protect and care for his female companions. You must allow me to play out my role.'

'I wouldn't dream of denying you that,' Nell said wryly. She was rather enjoying this strange anonymity. It felt as if they were starting with a clean page. Two people who had only just met, who brought with them none of the ghosts from the past... One night...one anonymous night...

She waved to Molly and Marianna as their boat sped away, and then turned back to confront her striking companion. 'So, where will you take me, kind sir?'

'To dress you,' Luca said, his lips curving wickedly.

CHAPTER NINE

THE costume shop belonging to one of Luca's friends was located in one of the narrow alleyways behind the square. It was dark inside like a warm cave full of jewels, but the jewels were silk, and the silk was cut cunningly to make the most of the female form.

Nell gasped as she saw herself in the ruby-red gown Luca had picked out for her. The bodice left nothing to the imagination, but she felt exposed in a very feminine way, a way that prompted her to ease her breasts a little further out from the cruelly laced bodice.

'It has to be tight, *signora*,' the shop owner explained to her in the dressing room, 'to make the most of your bosom.'

Well, it certainly did that. Did all Venetians have such a knowing way with them, Nell wondered, or was that just another product of the magic that was carnival? There was a transparent lace fichu peeping out at the front of the bodice of the dress, and that was all that stood between her and total exposure. Her nipples were on fire, the blood rushing to them thanks to the boned and laced top, and every time she eased her shoulders in a shrug they were straining to escape. So she wouldn't be doing that, Nell determined.

Her waist looked minute, her bosom huge, her feet tiny in

the high-heeled satin slippers. The dress rustled as she moved, causing the air around her to rise up bringing with it an age-old mix of perfumes. She felt as if she had been transported to another time, another world, where anything was possible…

'You should use this mask now, and carry a fan,' the owner advised. 'And a beauty spot just here,' she added, placing a small black patch on Nell's cheekbone beneath the fabulous white silk mask studded with rhinestone and pearl she was wearing in place of the Columbine mask. The woman had dressed her hair in the style she had so admired. It was held up with diamanté combs at each side and fell in soft curls around her face.

The owner stood back to admire her protégé. 'You look beautiful, *signora*… like a true lady of the court.'

'That's how I feel,' Nell admitted, smiling as she examined her greatly changed reflection in the looking glass. 'Like a lady of the court.' A wicked lady, she added to herself silently, pursing her lips to add some rouge.

'Would you like to show the gentleman who brought you here now?' the woman invited. Nell knew that she had opened the shop especially for them at Luca's request, but like Luca she was playing the game of anonymity to the hilt.

With a last glance over her shoulder at the fascinating stranger in the looking glass, Nell inclined her head.

He was stunned when she came through the door. It was fortunate that his role in this drama demanded that he dip her a low bow. His feelings were so close to the surface, so raw and unconfined, he was glad of his mask as well as the shadows in the intimate boutique. 'You look beautiful, *signora*… The costume becomes you.' His arm tingled beneath the touch of Nell's small, pale hand. 'Shall we continue the adventure?'

As he stared into her eyes he could see them darkening

behind the mask. But there was a warmth between them now he found as addictive as the lust. And she was beautiful, perhaps the most beautiful woman in the history of carnival. And she was his.

The music had slowed to more sensuous rhythms by the time they returned to the square; the old people and the children had long since gone to their beds. But for the beautiful young woman in her ruby-red gown and her striking companion, a tall, powerful figure dressed all in black, the night had just begun.

'Would you like a glass of champagne?'

'I'd love one.'

'Then we shall call in at *Ai Tosi* and arrange for our own supply.'

'Instead of coffee?' Nell suggested drily.

'Coffee?' Her masked companion looked askance.

'Carnival?' she whispered, guessing what was in his mind.

'You're learning,' he murmured.

She hadn't expected a waiter to set up an ice bucket for them in the square and then stand guard over it. 'This is such an incredible night.'

'No, it's carnival,' the masked man at her side corrected her, whispering in her ear so she shivered involuntarily. Taking her hand, he twirled her round slowly, sensuously in front of him. 'And now we dance...'

His touch shimmered down her naked arms, making her quiver in delicious anticipation. There was so much of her that was covered, and so much that was revealed. But her eyes were bold now. As they stepped onto the dance floor she felt all the constraints forced upon her by modern convention disappear. The high-heeled shoes tipped her hips at an inviting angle and the gown thrust her breasts out on display. Even the steps she was taking, tiny, controlled, modest, were a reminder of the forces simmering so near the surface. This was a new world, a time out of time, where they were simply two people, one man and one woman, who found themselves in a setting designed for intrigue and romance.

As the beat of the music grew faster their movements became stronger and more passionate. It was as if they were playing out all their deepest thoughts and desires in moves and flashing looks born of the moment, with no stain from the past to dilute them. Nothing could hold them back; they were aware of nothing but each other; all that stood between them now was the truth. It was attraction at its purest and most physically intense. It transcended all the value judgements they might have made in that other world where carnival held no sway. Could there be a greater escape, a greater rush than this? Nell wondered, as her dark companion tipped her so low over his arm that her hair brushed the ground. Sweeping her up again, he brought her close, so their lips were almost touching at the end of the dance.

'Are you thirsty?'

All her appetites were raging, and thirst was only one of them. She nodded.

'Come with me and we'll find a quiet spot.'

He took her to a bench in the shadows, where they could see without being seen. Like a wraith the waiter approached with iced flutes, which he filled with champagne.

'That will be all, thank you.'

She sat back as her handsome companion dismissed the waiter, and she prepared to sip the golden liquid.

'No!'

The command was soft, but forceful.

'No?'

'This is how we drink…' Twining his arm around hers, he brought his own glass to her lips to feed her with the sparkling liquid.

She reciprocated, steadying the delicate rim against the full swell of his bottom lip.

'Now drink,' he murmured.

She held his gaze as she obeyed. As a drop fell onto the full swell of her bosom, he dipped his head and licked it away. She drew in a fast breath of surprise, of delight—the touch of his tongue, a little rough and very knowing, was so stimulating. Easing her shoulders back, she made sure that he had a nipple to attend to next...

'Lady, you will be compromised,' he warned, pulling away.

She pouted, missing the delicious sensation, feeling it as an ache between her legs that forced her to ease her position on the stone bench without even knowing that she did so. But he saw.

'There is an answer to your problem...'

'Tell me,' she instructed.

'There was a time when a lady's honour was worth more than a man's life. And so, in order to progress a relationship forged on the briefest of meetings without unpleasant consequences, a way was devised to...accommodate a gentleman's companion.'

'Accommodate?' She tasted the word.

'I don't touch you...you don't touch me.'

'Oh.'

'And you're already disappointed.' His lips tugged up in wry appreciation. She didn't answer.

'Sit forward a little and then lean back against the bench and let your legs fall open...'

She did as he said, excitement racing through her at the thought of doing something so wicked... But what?

'I want you to close your eyes and imagine you are wearing no underwear. Close them,' he ordered, when her eyes widened in surprise at his suggestion. 'That's good. Now imagine you have one leg over my shoulder, and you are quite exposed…the cool evening breeze is tantalising you, and you long to be touched…'

Desperately aroused, she moistened her lips, her ears keenly tuned to hear his next instruction.

'And now I'm touching you…just those lush, swollen lips…one finger on each, massaging gently. It's so good, and you sigh, but it isn't enough. It only reminds you of the place I'm not touching…the place that seems more swollen and needy than anywhere else… But I'm cruel, I ignore it…'

His chanting voice never rose higher than a whisper, but he might have been giving her the sternest of instruction. Her hips were working against the silken folds of her gown as if he were indeed touching her.

'That's good,' he murmured approvingly, 'that's very good. So good in fact, I'm going to reward you…'

A cry escaped her throat and she opened her legs a little wider.

'Yes, I'm watching you. You've opened your legs so wide for me, and I'm looking at you now very closely. I can see that you're swollen, and moist, and ready for me. I can see your muscles contracting and relaxing, I can feel your heat…and now my finger has found you—'

She cried out, clutching the bench to steady herself, while he made quieting sounds.

'I know which side you like the best… I know how to rest my finger there and stroke gently but persuasively—'

A sound escaped her throat. She was close, so close…

'I'm rubbing now…a little faster, and with more pressure. You like it…you like it very much. You are bucking against me, urging me on…calling to me, ordering me… That's right…that's right,' he soothed, when she moaned her encouragement. 'Your cheeks are flushed; your breathing rapid… I'm going to hold you now, because in another few passes of my finger you're going to be there and I have to catch you when you fall…'

She shrieked as he tipped her over the edge, writhing on the bench in the throes of the most extreme pleasure she had ever known. It went on and on, and he held her firmly in his arms, smothering her guttural cries in the folds of his cloak.

Until that moment, he hadn't touched her once.

'There, my lady, isn't that better? And no damage done. Even an irate father, or some other man who might think he has a claim on you, can have no complaint. You have done nothing wrong other than throw yourself into the spirit of carnival.'

'How convenient.' A sensuous smile curved her lips. 'Do you have many such celebrations here in Venice, sir?'

'As many as you like,' he promised softly, holding her gaze.

But the dream couldn't last forever. A sombre mood fell over them as they left the little shop. Nell, in her everyday clothes again, was unmasked, though she carried with her the beautiful Columbine mask Luca had bought for her. She clutched it as if in some way it could help her to hold on to the fantasy. But it was just a fantasy, and as such it was already fading.

When they boarded Luca's boat he went immediately to loosen the mooring ropes, leaving Nell on her own in the cabin. He was distant, changed, not the wicked gallant she had spent the evening with. Now he was preoccupied, purposeful and once again remote.

The sleek white craft had a history she preferred to forget. It only taunted her with the knowledge that Luca could arouse her at will. She wondered now if it had all been play-acting for him. He had removed his costume to steer the boat home and the black jeans and shirt he wore beneath seemed like a brazen statement of his masculinity—a cruel reminder of how much she wanted him.

She was glad he didn't ask her to join him in the cockpit.

She still couldn't believe what had happened, or that she had let herself go to such an extent—and in public! Anyone might have seen them! Except that, as Luca said, they had done nothing wrong, and he had not touched her.

He was an incredible man—incredible and untouchable. He always kept part of himself detached and distant, safe inside his fortress without a gate.

Left alone with her thoughts, Nell stared back across the lagoon at the twinkling carnival lights. They were receding into the distance, and finally they disappeared. She turned again to look at Luca as he opened up the throttle. The sudden surge of power made her pulse race. It took so little—he seemed to have beguiled her into a permanent state of arousal. But at least she was able to study him from the safety of the cabin: the chiselled profile, the powerful forearms braced against the wheel, muscle and sinew clearly delineated in the moonlight…

She was so engrossed in her appreciative inspection that she didn't realise the Columbine mask was slipping from her lap until she heard it clatter to the floor. As she bent to pick it up she felt him look at her.

'Are you all right?'

'I dropped my mask.'

'Yes, I know that…'

She knew his words were double-edged, and it was true, she had dropped her mask, but then so had he. And now? Now she was angry with herself, because nothing had changed, and it seemed nothing could stop her wanting him. And they still hadn't even kissed properly yet.

Was it all a game to him? All she wanted was a moment's tenderness, a kiss, a tender kiss…and she wanted that so badly that even her pride wasn't enough to brush the need aside.

Why couldn't she face up to the truth? Luca didn't have a tender bone in his body. If she waited for a tender kiss she'd wait forever. But on the bright side, Nell reflected ironically, she could have the most incredible and inventive sex with him any time she liked.

'I wish you hadn't bought these.' She stared at the mask, knowing it had become the butt of her ill humour, but all the anger inside her had to find an outlet somewhere.

'I couldn't let you inflict that ugly thing on Molly. And I could hardly leave you out.'

'I was trying to teach Molly something.'

'You can do too much preaching where children are concerned. I think it's better if you point them in the direction they should go. Then with a little encouragement and guidance—'

'And you know so much about children?'

'I've treated a lot of them, yes.' Slowing the boat as they approached the city limit, Luca glanced at her over his shoulder. 'The first time we met I thought you smothered her.'

Instantly the air was full of ugly, unspoken words. That was how it always was between them. They were like two fires raging out of control, meeting in a furious clash of fractured hopes and damaged dreams. In the end they always burned each other out.

'Think about what I've said, Nell...'

His parting shot before turning back to steer the boat made her fury rise, but, since she was unable to retaliate, it gave her chance to consider what he had said more carefully. After Jake's accident Molly had become the centre of her universe—and that was a lot of attention focused on one small child.

'You really think I smother her?' she called out to him. She had to know.

'You can't cover a green shoot with compost, however rich in nutrients, and expect it to grow. You have to let the shoot see the sun from time to time.'

She didn't really want to hear that, Nell discovered. 'Please don't patronise me—and for goodness' sake, spare me the psychology!'

'So you can go on making the same mistakes?'

'We're talking about *my* daughter. The way I bring up Molly is my business. It's got nothing to do with you.'

'So I should have let her wear that ugly plague mask when there are so many more attractive possibilities?'

Their voices had become raised, and as they drifted in towards the hotel mooring Nell finally snapped. 'Oh, you're right! You're always right!'

'Not always, Nell,' Luca assured her in a low voice. 'Just most of the time where you're concerned.'

CHAPTER TEN

MOLLY was still tired at breakfast the next day, but her face lit up every time she mentioned Luca. And she just wouldn't stop talking about him. Nell bore it the best she could, smiling, listening attentively, struggling to keep her own feelings under wraps. She couldn't help but notice that Molly carried the mask he had bought for her everywhere she went.

Why hadn't she thought to buy one as fanciful and delicious? It was exactly the type of thing she would have adored when she was Molly's age. Instead, she had picked out something 'worthy', something she thought Molly would learn from. But Luca was right about that at least; there were many different ways of learning…

When the phone rang, Nell answered it absently, still watching with concern as Molly picked half-heartedly at her food. 'Luca?' She practically sprang to attention, but then she noticed that Molly was watching her and carefully relaxed.

'Nell. Are you still there?'

'I haven't forgotten our meeting.'

'I'm not calling about a meeting.'

'Oh?' There was an ache in her chest so real she was rubbing it, Nell realised, pulling her hand away. One night with a man in a mask did not a romance make! When would she face reality and accept things for what they were? And she really should thank him again for the masks—

'I'm not calling about the masks either,' he said as if he had read her mind. There was a smile in his voice. She almost wished he would use his cold, remote voice. It would be easier to deal with. She had seen another side of him, a warm, amusing, sensual side, and she wanted to claim it, hold it tight…

'I'm calling to apologise,' he said.

'What?' Stunned, Nell looked at Molly. 'Could you give me a moment?'

'I'll go and find Marianna.' Molly skidded to a halt by the door. 'And Mum?'

'Yes?'

'Can you tell Luca I said thank you for the mask?'

'Of course.' Nell waited with her hand over the receiver until Molly had left the room.

'Are you still there?'

'Yes.'

'I wanted to say that it was wrong of me to interfere between you and Molly last night.'

Fighting to keep her breath steady, she managed, 'Forget it.'

'That's just it. I can't forget it, and I want to make it up to you both.'

'That's really not necessary.'

'You'll have to forgive me if I disagree. My sister's children are staying with me while she's away with her husband, and I thought it would be an ideal opportunity for Molly to meet some kids her own age.'

No, she couldn't do this…not even for Molly. 'But she doesn't speak Italian.' That was a starting point. She'd think up some more excuses as she went along.

'The language won't be a problem—children have their

own language,' Luca assured her. 'And of course, you and Marianna would be welcome to come along too.'

'I said Marianna could have some time off—'

'Molly will be quite safe here at the house, then. My mother's staying over too.'

'Your mother?'

As Nell mulled it over Luca added, 'I think Molly enjoyed herself last night. She should experience the real Venice while she has the chance.'

Nell hated it when he was right.

'Well, what do you think of the idea?'

Molly would love being with children her own age, Nell reflected. It was just what she needed.

'So, what do you say?'

As Molly's wistful face flashed into Nell's mind, she realised there was only one thing she could say.

'Thank you. We'd love to come.' For an only child, the opportunity Luca had proposed was like gold dust.

'Is this Luca's house?' Molly stared up at the grand façade.

'I suppose it must be.' Nell followed Molly's gaze. She knew some people would only see the dilapidation in Venice, but what she saw was history and the accumulated talent of craftsmen across the ages displayed on every corner. 'It's like a living museum.'

'I love it here, Mum.'

'So do I,' Nell admitted wistfully. She'd come a long way from hating Venice. She rapped on a brass knocker in the shape of a lion's head and after a minute or so an elderly gentleman opened the door.

When they walked into the vaulted hall it was as if they had stepped back in time. Nell suspected that the frescoes on the ceiling panels and on the walls must be originals that had been restored. It was cool and shady and very beautiful, with lush palms thriving in ornate pots.

'They love the shade.'

They turned to see an elegant older woman entering the hallway through one of the tall archways. Her heels clipped on the marble floor as she came towards them.

'*Buon giorno!* Hello! I saw you looking at them,' she explained to Nell, indicating the tall plants with a graceful gesture. '*Grazie*, Paolo. I will take charge now. *Bellissima!*' she exclaimed, dipping to cup Molly's face in slender beringed hands. 'I am delighted you decided to spend the day with me.'

Molly's face broke into a smile as she stared up. 'You're the lady from last night—the lady who took our photograph.'

'Forgive me. I should have introduced myself then, but I didn't want to intrude. I am your friend's mother.' Smiling, she turned to offer her hand in greeting to Nell. 'Forgive me. Our lives revolve around children in Italy.'

Nell returned the smile as they shook hands. She was almost as entranced as Molly—except by the reference to their 'friend'! What had Luca told his mother?

'I've heard all about you,' Luca's mother was explaining to Molly. 'And my grandchildren can't wait to meet you. They're in the garden now.' She held out her hand, which Molly took without hesitation.

So Luca had been with his mother the previous evening. Which shouldn't have mattered to Nell, except she found that it did…a great deal. 'Did Luca explain that we have a meeting today?' She glanced at Molly.

'Don't worry, Nell—may I call you Nell? Molly will be happy here at the *palazzo*. And as for your meeting…' His mother's smile widened. 'I've told Luca I think it's such a good thing you're doing I'm going to ask you if you will consider me as one of your volunteers.'

Nell's eyes widened with surprise. 'I'd love to talk to you about it.' She hadn't expected to find support in such an unexpected quarter.

'Then we'll talk just as soon as you finish your meeting with Luca.'

The mother was almost as persuasive as the son, Nell thought wryly. Then they noticed the elderly retainer hovering by the door.

'*Mi scusi, Contessa Barbaro...*'

'*Si*, Paolo. Please tell the children that Molly and I will be with them shortly. They are so impatient, you know,' she said, turning back to Nell.

As Molly mouthed, 'Countess?' Nell shrugged discreetly, and then tensed. She didn't need to turn around to know that Luca was behind her; she could feel his energy lapping over her.

'Mother...'

'*Bello!*'

'Molly.' With a small bow, he greeted Molly formally with a handshake.

As he turned to greet her, Nell realised that all the tiny hairs had risen in unison on the back of her neck.

'Molly and I were just leaving, *bello*. We'll speak again soon, Nell, I hope?'

'I'm looking forward to it.'

'What's this, a conspiracy?' Luca asked drily.

'Your mother has offered her services as a volunteer.' Nell found it hard to hide her satisfaction, or to quell her memories of the previous night.

'Has she, now?' Luca's gaze followed the sound of heels disappearing into the distance.

'Well, I'm ready to start. Where are we meeting?' The sooner they concentrated on business, the better!

'The meeting's been cancelled.'

'By whom?'

'By me.'

She stared at him. 'I don't understand.'

'I don't see that we need a formal meeting at this stage. We can talk just as well here.'

'Here?'

'Why not here?' His rugged features softened into a smile.

Luca could be extremely charming when it suited him, Nell thought, struggling to remain immune. But when one corner of his mouth tugged up as it was doing now it made such an attractive crease down one side of his face, and his eyes…

'I thought you might like the grand tour first,' he suggested, reclaiming her attention with a jolt. 'It's rather an interesting old house.'

And not the only thing that had caught her interest, Nell mused drily, keeping her thoughts to herself. But was it wise to be investigating the furthest reaches of some ancient palace with a man she had such strong feelings for?

With his mother about, and the elderly servant moving on silent feet who knew where… Yes, it would be fine, she concluded. 'Thank you, I'd love to see round.'

Luca led the way up the stairs. Except they weren't stairs as Nell knew them, but more like something out of a Busby Berkeley movie spectacular, with a magnificent sweeping marble staircase that had a grand piano tucked beneath its curve. 'Impressive…'

'Don't get too carried away,' Luca warned wryly. 'This place is huge, and it's a huge responsibility too—not to mention a huge drain on my pocket. But as it's been passed down the generations…' He eased his shoulders in a shrug. 'I do all the heavy restoration work myself, only calling in the experts when I need craftsmen for the stone carvings, or for the frescoes.' He glanced at the ceiling she had so admired.

'You don't mind acting as labourer?' He was more than equal to the task, but she was surprised to think of him loading stone onto his shoulders or ripping away rotten wood with his bare hands.

'I consider it a privilege. I happen to think this is a cause worth fighting for, and it brings me closer to the past, to the people who built this place, and my ancestors who lived here.' With a rueful smile he peeled a piece of plaster from the wall.

'But it's a never-ending task?' Nell guessed.

'Like painting your Forth Bridge in Great Britain?'

As he smiled a bolt of heat shot through her, and it wasn't just lust—it was something that left her feeling far more vulnerable than that.

'The relatives.' Luca nodded, indicating the life-sized portraits hanging on the walls above their heads.

'From the year dot?' Nell almost smiled too as their eyes met briefly.

'And beyond,' he assured her.

What was happening to her…to them? Tucking a wayward strand of hair behind her ear, Nell forced herself to concentrate as Luca started to give her a potted history of the house. In spite of everything, were they starting to like each other? They'd had the worst of starts, but last night she had seen a different side to him. Apart from the sensuality, he had been light-hearted, fun, full of enthusiasm for the traditions and history of his country. And now she had discovered a deeper side—a side she would never have guessed at; a side that belied Luca's stylish outer shell and revealed a man who didn't mind getting his hands dirty, who cared deeply about his heritage, his family, the things that really mattered…

'At the moment, of course, this place is only a work in progress, not yet a home.'

Was this the same cold-hearted individual talking now, the

man she thought she knew? 'Well, I think it's beautiful,' Nell said honestly, 'and well worth fighting for.'

'I camp out in a few rooms at the top. Would you like to see them?'

'I'd love to.' Her enthusiasm was burgeoning and she was intrigued to see how he lived. Following Luca across the landing, Nell ducked her head as they started up a second, much narrower flight of stairs.

'This is the attic, which used to be the servants' quarters before I moved in. But now this is my mother's room, these are the children's rooms, the nursery…'

As they moved on, Nell was sure he couldn't have surprised her more. Each room was meticulously restored with each ancient architectural feature intact.

'And finally, this is my room.'

It overlooked the canal, with light spilling through the open windows. 'Oh, Luca, it's beautiful!' The view drew Nell to the balcony, where she looked out over the canal. Suddenly she realised what she was doing. 'I'm so sorry—I should have waited to be invited in.'

'Go right ahead.'

Walking up to the stone balustrade, Nell rested her arms on it and allowed herself, just for a moment, to imagine what it might be like to call such a place home. Did Luca know how fortunate he was? Yes, she thought he did.

'It's like a Canaletto painting come to life.' She felt a tremble of awareness, and knew that he was right behind her.

'I'm glad you like it.'

As he trailed one fingertip down her naked arm, she turned. 'No, Luca.'

'No?' His lips curved in the way she could never resist.

'No.' She walked a few steps away from him. She'd burned her fingers for the last time. She couldn't switch on and then off again as Luca seemed able to do. 'We're going to be working together, so I hope…'

'That we can be friends?'

She nodded, pressing her lips down wryly as she prepared to drive a wedge between them. 'Friends, yes, but lovers?' She shook her head. Insanely, for a moment, she hoped he would disagree, drag her to him and kiss away her doubts. But, as he hadn't kissed her yet, and she had hardly given him the best of encouragement, it wasn't likely that situation was about to change now.

She wasn't surprised when he turned away and started pointing out the various sights that made Venice the city it was. There wasn't anything in Luca's expression to suggest that he was disappointed by her stand. Perhaps as a man he was programmed to make a move, and just couldn't help himself. Or perhaps he wasn't particularly concerned about her refusal. And if that was the case, shouldn't she be glad? Wasn't that safer?

The only difficulty with her resolution to remain aloof from Luca, Nell discovered later, was that man might be programmed to mate, but so was woman. She was sitting outside in the garden with his mother, watching the children play. Luca, who was on call, had been paged by the hospital. It had brought their encounter on the balcony to an abrupt halt, which she suspected was a relief to both of them.

Luca's balcony had been off a sitting room the size of a small ballroom. She guessed his bedroom would be somewhere beyond that. The *palazzo* was so vast, and his quarters so isolated, no one would have known if they had lingered in his room. But far better for her that things had turned out the way they had.

'These times are the best, don't you think, my dear?'

Nell turned her head as the *contessa* began to speak. They were enjoying some welcome shade beneath a bleached linen parasol, reclining on identical deep-cushioned sunbeds. 'Midday?' Nell wrinkled her nose, not liking to disagree—but it was scorching hot.

'I'm talking about dream-time, Nell, when we let our minds fly free.'

Nell stiffened. Dream-time? How much had the *contessa* guessed about her relationship with Luca? She played it safe, humming a non-committal answer, and tried to distract herself by concentrating on the children. She started to smile. Luca had been right about them finding their own language...

'Stolen times.'

The *contessa* wasn't about to give up, Nell reflected wryly. The older woman was definitely on a reconnaissance mission. Nell decided to act innocent. 'Stolen times?'

'They're the sweetest of all, don't you think?'

The *contessa* made everything sound so deliciously decadent. Tipping her sunglasses down her nose, Nell tried not to smile. 'I'm not sure I understand what you mean.'

'Don't tell me you wouldn't rather be somewhere else right now.'

'Well, I suppose...' Luca's bedroom sprang mischievously into her mind.

'I hardly know you, and yet I feel instinctively that you should relax and spoil yourself more frequently.' The *contessa* rose up a fraction on the sunbed and turned her head to look at Nell. 'I hope you don't mind me speaking my mind like this?'

'No, of course not.' What else could she say with the *contessa*'s gaze soldered to her face?

'Good, I'm glad you agree.' The *contessa* sat up, all business now. 'I would like to invite you to dinner tonight— with Molly, of course, and Marianna.'

What, and see Luca again? 'No. I mean, I'm afraid that won't be possible tonight, Contessa.'

'Not possible?'

Nell saw some of her son's iron resolve in the *contessa*'s imperious cobalt stare. 'I have a lot of work to do before our meeting. I mean, I know it's been delayed, but—' Nell knew she was flailing and wasn't surprised when the *contessa* flashed back.

'*But?* You must have prepared for the meeting you were supposed to hold this morning?'

'That's true…' Nell was up against an immovable force, and she knew it.

'Well, then? Molly is happy, as you can see.' The *contessa* gestured towards the small playground, where Molly and an older child had taken charge of the smaller children on the swings. 'She can stay here and play with my grandchildren, while you return to the hotel to prepare for dinner…' The confidence in the older woman's voice began to fade as Nell stood up decisively.

'That's very kind of you, but I really can't accept,' she said firmly. How could she remain under the same roof as Luca and act as though there were nothing between them? Their encounter on his balcony, coupled with the way her thoughts had strayed while she was in his home, meant she had to keep her distance. 'I'll fetch Molly now—'

'But there is no reason to take her home yet. Why don't you let her stay the night?'

'I wouldn't dream of putting you to so much trouble.'

'Trouble? Nonsense!' the *contessa* exclaimed, waving her hands for emphasis. 'If my grandchildren are happy that is all I care about. You will be doing an old lady a very great favour. Please. And you must come to dinner so you can say goodnight to her.'

'Well…'

'I would enjoy it so much, and so would Molly.'

Checkmate, Nell realised wryly, mentally knocking her king onto its side. 'I'll just make sure Molly's OK with that.'

'Of course…' There was a faint smile playing around the *contessa*'s lips as Nell hurried away.

By the time she got back to the hotel Nell had changed her mind again. Molly was a confident child who didn't need tucking in; if she was to stay the night with the *contessa*, there was no reason for Nell to return to the *palazzo* for dinner.

'But the water taxi's on its way to pick you up,' Luca's mother protested when Nell called to excuse herself. 'Luca has just this moment returned from the hospital. Here, let me pass you over to him.'

'No, that's…' Nell started tapping her foot as she listened to the muffled exchanges between mother and son, and then tensed as Luca came on the line.

'Nell? Aren't you coming? Mother's expecting you.'

'I'm sure your mother will understand.'

At the other end of the phone, Luca quickly clutched at another straw and held on to it. 'But it's my mother's…' He calculated quickly. '…sixtieth birthday.' He had to cover the mouthpiece to smother the indignant sound sailing across the room. 'You don't want to ruin it for her, do you?'

'Your mother didn't say anything about it being a special occasion!'

'Well, she wouldn't, would she?'

And have her think she must bring a gift? Probably not. 'But your mother hardly knows me. Surely she won't miss me at the celebration.'

'You made quite an impression…'

'That much of an impression?' Her voice was ironic.

'No, I suppose you're right.' He played it straight. 'But it is her birthday and I want everything to be perfect for her. Mothers, eh? What can you do?'

'Don't you have any scruples at all?'

Luca let the silence hang. He didn't know about his scruples, but he did have to see Nell again—and not just for sex. Since the carnival the lasting impressions in his mind had been coloured by a woman he desired, a woman he enjoyed being with, a woman whose smile he could never forget. In the same way he could never forget what fun she was when she was truly relaxed, or how she laughed, or the way she was with Molly, and even her consideration for Marianna. He had snapshots in his head right now—all of them of Nell. The sex was extraordinary between them, but so was the hunger he felt just to be with her again.

'May I tell Mother to expect you?'

Nell ground her jaw. 'Tell the *contessa* that I'm looking forward to it.'

Luca's lips curved in a smile as he cut the line.

Nell had spent some time at the dinner explaining to the *contessa* the pivotal role she hoped Luca would play in the scheme, and how she needed him. She wasn't the only one who could use her wiles, and if bringing the *contessa* on board proved to be the key to Luca's co-operation, she'd go flat out to make sure it happened.

Yes, she needed him, and in how many ways? Nell wondered as the *contessa* took up the banner for her and started trying to persuade her son to forget about pilot schemes and make the voluntary service a permanent fixture at the hospital immediately. Luca didn't comment, or argue as he usually did, but sank his face into his hand to stare at Nell as if her project was the last thing on his mind.

It was the last thing on Nell's mind too. It felt so good just being in Luca's home. His masculinity invaded even the air they breathed as well as her body, and her mind. He had baited the hook and she had swallowed it gladly. She wanted to talk to him, to learn everything about him; she wanted time with him, time that wasn't tainted by duty or by lust. Having begun the process of getting to know him, she was hungry for more, even though she knew how dangerous that was.

Raising her damask napkin to her lips, Nell took a few moments out to escape the dark eyes drilling into her. She couldn't, she mustn't fall in love with him. After Jake, how could she trust her own judgement?

'So you will agree to this, *bello?*'

Nell refocused to see Luca's shoulders move in an easy shrug. 'I can refuse you nothing.' The *contessa* seemed reassured.

He was agreeing? To what? What had she missed? Nell was suddenly acutely aware of everything around her.

'So, Nell.' Luca turned to her. 'Do you think we will be able to work together successfully?'

Had he agreed to everything while she had been day-dreaming? Nell wondered. Maybe not, but it looked as though they were a giant step closer to coming to an agreement, thanks to his mother. But how would she find working with Luca on a daily basis? Would she be able to handle it—to keep him at a distance, keep her thoughts in check? Would she be able to stop Molly thinking this working arrangement might lead to something more?

Molly was waiting for her answer with as much, if not more interest than Luca and his mother, Nell realised, ago-nising over the reply she should make. The voluntary scheme meant a lot to her, but Molly meant infinitely more.

'I'll be back at school soon, so we won't be here forever,' Molly was pointing out.

That was true. And this was everything she'd hoped for. She had to get over her personal concerns and give it a chance. 'Welcome to the team.' Nell raised her glass.

'To our closer association,' Luca answered, holding her gaze.

But just at the moment when she should have been suffused with triumph, Nell's anxiety levels rose. As they brought their crystal goblets together in a toast she couldn't help noticing the barely contained excitement in Molly's eyes. It complicated everything.

'Paolo was looking tired, so I brought your coat out,' Luca explained in answer to Nell's unspoken question. She was standing in the hallway waiting for the elderly servant to bring the coat and show her out. She had been hoping to slip away while Luca had been detained by a call from the hospital. Marianna was staying over to help the *contessa* with the children, which to Nell's mind had seemed to leave everything tied up neatly—until now.

'Why didn't you tell me you were leaving?' Luca demanded.

'I didn't want to disturb you. And Paolo very kindly called a taxi for me—'

'A taxi?' Luca stared at her. 'So you were going to leave without saying goodbye to me?'

She opened her mouth, but only a half-sigh of apology came out.

'Surely you knew I would take you back?'

'I didn't think…' Nell's voice tailed away as Luca's gaze remained on her face. 'Look, there's really no need for you to take me back. The water taxi will be here in a minute.'

'There's every need. Do you think I would let you return to the hotel on your own at night when my boat's moored outside the door?'

'I'll be fine, honestly.'

'Nell, whatever's happened between us, we can still be friends. We have to be if we're going to be working together.'

The threat was light, but it was there. *'Bene.'* She slipped into Italian, using a word she had heard on numerous occasions—some of those occasions when people had thrown up their hands and caved in. With so much to lose, it seemed appropriate now.

'Complimenti!' Luca murmured wryly. 'You have another word of Italian.'

'Are you mocking me?'

'Would I?'

She refused to look at him. She would not look at him and see the humour she knew would be in Luca's eyes—the humour that always won her over.

'Imagine how improved your language skills would be if you decided to stay in Venice.'

Was he teasing? 'I won't be here long enough for that,' she assured him.

As he opened the door Nell wondered if she would ever get used to the sight in front of her. The view was extraordinary; opening the door like raising the curtain on some sumptuous theatrical production. Unlike most other canals the life of the dark water in Venice was dictated by the closeness of the open sea and tidal flats. It moved sinuously in a constant pattern of restless waves so that even Luca's large launch swayed lazily in the current beside the landing stage. And just a few yards further along the bank, Nell realised, was the spot where they had first met.

She hugged herself, knowing she had to divide her life into boxes, or she'd never come through this visit to Venice in one piece. The only way she could do it was by maintaining a professional relationship with the man who had saved Molly's life, the man who could make her scheme a success.

'You're remembering, aren't you?'

Luca's voice was gentle. He had turned to watch her as she stared out across the water. The cobbled *calle* where they had stood all those years ago was grazed by moonlight, illuminating the exact spot where Luca had stood with Molly in his arms...and there were the steps where she had stumbled...

'You must look to the future, Nell,' he said gently. 'For your sake as well as for Molly's.'

Nell turned without comment to board the launch. It was no use fooling herself. She knew their future was none of Luca's concern.

CHAPTER ELEVEN

NELL spent the morning at the hospital, learning the ropes, observing the way things were done. Each place she visited had its own take on what constituted a smooth-running operation, and it was crucial that she knew what that was in Luca's hospital so that she could avoid treading on anyone's toes. By the time the volunteers were ready to go in she would have everything prepared for them, from a map of the building to a list of staff names.

She was about to leave when Luca stopped her by the door. 'I'd like to take you to lunch.'

'Lunch?' Alarm bells started up.

'There are a few more points I'd like to discuss…'

And hadn't she fallen for that before?

'I'm serious, Nell,' Luca insisted, as if reading her mind.

Nell's heart gave a doleful thud as she realised that he was. And in spite of all her brave assertions, she was disappointed.

'It shouldn't take long—Nell? Do you need me to phrase my offer some other way?'

'No, no. I'm sorry.' Her eyes cleared as she stared up at him, but her thoughts were still far away. 'Lunch should be OK.'

He frowned. Nell guessed he suspected she was thinking out loud, and not simply about dining arrangements.

'So shall we go?' he pressed.

There was a touch of impatience in his voice, but she could see nothing remotely predatory in his gaze. 'If you feel it would be helpful.'

'I do.'

He had managed to secure a table for them at the most romantic restaurant in Venice. When Nell moved in front of him to sit down he caught a waft of her scent. It reminded him of a spring meadow—it reminded him to cool down. Though how he was supposed to do that when the temperature was soaring inside as well as out, he had no idea. Thunderclouds were threatening over the San Marco Basin like an oppressive scene-setter for some dramatic encounter. He had to hope their lunch date would be spared the fireworks. He wanted to talk, to get to know her, to relax... something both of them found equally difficult to engineer time for.

'How do you do that?' he murmured as she slid into the booth.

'How do I do what?' She glanced at him, just the briefest eye contact, and then looked away as if she didn't trust herself to hold his gaze.

'How do you look so cool when everyone else in Venice is at melting point?'

She smiled faintly. 'That's funny.'

'Funny?'

'I used to think that about you.' She shrugged. 'Maybe I've grown used to the heat...become used to dressing for it more sensibly.'

The comment drew his attention to the elegant, loose-fitting dress she had on, one of a selection she had taken to wearing for work in place of a suit. She looked beautiful.

She stiffened when she caught him staring at her. 'Should we call for menus?' she suggested.

She was all business, keeping him at arm's length. He couldn't blame her for that. She knew as well as he did that there was always an unlit fuse between them…a fuse which common sense dictated neither one of them should ignite. *A few points to go over?* Had he really used that line again? His technique was slipping badly.

Except that technique was redundant where Nell was concerned. All that seemed right when he was with her was openness and sincerity. Nell was different to any woman he had known; she defied analysis. She was unpredictable: defensive, strong, yet so vulnerable. And more than a match for him.

Luca had found himself, uniquely, unsure of how to proceed. Instinct had always been enough to guide him in the past; he had certainly never planned a date with such precision before. He needed it to be a success.

'I think things are going well so far…' she started stiffly.

If this lunch was to remain neutral and friendly, he'd better get his mind in gear fast and think of something to say that was connected to her scheme. 'Yes…' He tried to refocus his mind, but his thoughts remained stubbornly single-track. He wanted a lot more than a business discussion with her.

It was a pretty interesting situation. He was sitting opposite the most desirable woman he had ever met, a woman he had already slept with, only to find that, having reached the goal, it wasn't enough—and nor was it the open-ended ticket he had supposed. If anything sex had made Nell more distant. She had retreated behind a barrier he didn't know how to breach. But he would breach it. He had to…if he was ever going to know her properly.

'We won't make too much of a call on your time once we are up and running.'

Her voice brought him back to full attention. 'I wouldn't have agreed to become part of this scheme of yours if I didn't want to be involved.' What was his alternative—not to see her?

'Just be sure you know what you're letting yourself in for, Luca—'

'I do know,' he cut across her. In truth, he wasn't sure of anything right now. But on this one point he could reassure her. 'I took charge of the family trust when I was twenty-five—'

'Around the time we first met?'

He gave a nod of assent.

Which might explain why he had taken himself so seriously, Nell conjectured. It was one hell of a responsibility. 'And the trust runs the hospital.'

'That's why I'm so protective of it,' Luca confirmed. 'That's where all my own spare cash goes…when it's not going into the house. Hospital first, house second.' He gave a rueful smile. 'They're both my life's work, as they were my father's. I made a promise to him before he died that I would carry on his work, and I have.'

The ache in Nell's chest grew worse. She didn't want to hear this. She didn't want to like him any more than she already did. She didn't want proof that he could be trusted, or had principles and strength of purpose…because that made it even harder not to fall in love with him.

He turned away to order wine.

'Just water for me, please. *Aqua naturale, per favore.*' She spoke directly to the waiter and could feel Luca's gaze burning into her.

'*Bene,*' he murmured approvingly. 'Won't you have one glass of wine?'

'I prefer to keep a clear head, if you don't mind. And I'll just have a starter. I have to get back to the hotel in…' Glancing at her wrist-watch, she exclaimed with surprise, 'Goodness, I didn't realise that was the time. I'm really sorry, Luca, but I'll have to leave here in about half an hour.'

The disappointment he felt was even worse than he could have imagined.

They had been working side by side for almost a week, and Luca had to admit Nell's voluntary scheme was working well. Hell! Even his mother was involved!

He stood watching for a while as Nell laughed at some joke she was sharing with one of his patients. Professionally speaking, his insistence that she should be part of the voluntary service on the ground was the best call he'd made in a long time. She was a natural; everyone loved her. But from a personal point of view it stank. She was under his gaze every day, forcing her delicious scent up his nostrils and making him watch her silky hair swinging round her shoulders as she walked her sassy walk. He had to observe her kindness at close quarters, share in her humour, witness her strength—all of which dug into him, reminding him what might have been if he had found his feelings a little sooner.

As it was, she barely noticed him when she was working. She was so busy—*too busy*. That was what she had said the first time he had invited her for coffee, and now she said it every time he asked, talking to him in a no-nonsense voice she apparently reserved for him alone. A voice that made him feel like a recalcitrant child who was getting under her feet—in his own hospital!

She could make time for everyone else, why not for him? What did he have to do to change things back to how they had used to be? Had he dreamed up the attraction between them? Only the constant ache in his groin reassured him that wasn't true...

And along with the purely physical ache, there was a

growing need for closeness on a very different level—and that was proving to be almost a bigger problem than the first. He didn't have any coping strategies for dealing with his emotional needs. How could he, when he'd never had any before?

He needed to woo her.

Woo her? Luca's lips pressed down as his inner voice came up with the suggestion. He'd been trying to do just that, not that he'd known where to begin—he hadn't had attempted to woo anyone since leaving school. He'd arranged a romantic meal, and made sure there were fresh flowers in her office. He'd taken the whole damn group of volunteers including Nell to a concert. He'd even contemplated queuing in the rain for tickets to one of the art galleries, before deciding that contracting pneumonia was contrary to all the accepted principles of seduction. As far as wooing went he had so far proved to be an abject failure.

Running a liberating finger beneath his collar, Luca stared out broodily through the window. Even the weather was against him.

'Luca?'

He looked round at her voice and watched her as she came swiftly across the ward towards him, smiling pleasantly. *Pleasantly!* He would have to take action soon.

He responded sensibly and professionally. 'Nell, hello.' He even curbed his smile, allowing himself just a small nod of approval. 'You're fitting in really well. And I thought you said your talent was for management, not hands-on?' He couldn't hold back the smile now, because it was true: she had made a real difference to morale on the wards.

When Luca smiled at her, hardly smiling really, more a slight tug at one corner of his mouth, but with so much challenge and humour in his voice, Nell wondered how she was staying so strong. Common sense, she told herself firmly, controlling the impulse to excitedly share everything she had learned that day. 'Oh, you know…' She flicked her wrist in a casual gesture. 'I'm really enjoying it. I like people.'

Luca's expression darkened. She didn't like *him*…not enough. 'How are the volunteers coming along? Are they ready to carry on without you yet?'

'Can't you wait to get rid of me?' she said wryly. 'I'd like to give them a couple more weeks.' She consciously diverted the conversation onto a practical track before Luca had chance to absorb her teasing remark. 'Your mother has offered to take over the pastoral side for me when I return home. She'll make an excellent superintendent for the scheme.'

His mother working—that had been another shock. Nell had certainly wrought some changes during her short stay in Venice.

'She can't wait to start,' she added.

He was shut out while his mother was in the loop. How had that happened? 'When did you say you were leaving?' he demanded.

'I didn't. But this was never going to be forever, Luca.'

As Nell held his gaze, Luca wondered how much pleasure she was getting from turning the tables on him. When they had first met he had wanted sex and nothing more. Then he'd discovered how much he enjoyed her company on a personal basis. Now he wanted to deepen the relationship, but she was holding out on him—making him pay. 'I know you have to leave,' he said impatiently. 'But don't you think you should tell me when?'

'I won't disappear without telling you.'

'Not like you tried to do after dinner that time?'

'Of course not. This is different.'

Was it? It only took a word, or a glance, for passion to flare between them, and now they were facing each other like contestants in the ring. 'Before you go I'll need to see your database of volunteers,' he pointed out, unnecessarily harshly. 'I shall want the names of everyone involved in the project so I can check up on them—particularly who's actually going to be in charge. And keep me up to speed in future, will you?' His unfocused anger was rising with every word.

'I'll be sure to release the necessary details so you can check up on your mother,' she told him drily. 'Or you could boot up your own computer, and hit "volunteer database". Relax, Luca. I'm not trying to hide anything from you. Your mother only confirmed today, and I haven't had chance to amend the records yet. Now, if you'll excuse me…'

'You're leaving?'

'I've finished my shift.'

'Let me see you to the door—'

'That's not necessary, Luca.' She held up her hand to stop him. 'I know my way out.'

It had been a long day on her feet and Nell was desperate to get away from Luca and back to the hotel. Confrontation with him always shook her up, made her ache for all the things she couldn't have. But for the first time since setting up the voluntary scheme she knew where she really belonged, and that was at the sharp end, dealing with people, not in the office. And it galled her to think that Luca appeared to know her better than she knew herself.

She lost herself with considerable relief amongst the press of people boarding the water-borne *vaporetto*. It was full of strangers going about their business, and at this moment she envied every one of them; they all seemed to know in which direction they were heading, which was more than she did. She was increasingly drawn to the richness of life in Italy, but she couldn't forget that her home was in England and that this was just a temporary stay. Perhaps one day she would be able to come back…

Gazing over her shoulder at the hospital building, Nell realised that Luca had made her reconsider her life and see things very differently. She should thank him for that—but from a safe distance, she reflected wryly.

Luca was like a band about to snap. There was something in the air… ions, electric particles, the sultry heat of Venice that made everything in the city slow to a crawl. Even the pigeons couldn't be bothered to fly, and had taken shelter beneath the seats on the Piazza San Marco, hoping for scraps. He couldn't concentrate in order to do his job properly. He couldn't seem to get on with anything. He couldn't manage without her.

He had to do something—something different, special, unique, to grab her interest. He wanted to start again from the beginning, get everything right this time, and then see how it panned out.

He found her sitting in the beautiful walled garden his mother had created before she gave him the *palazzo*. The two women were watching the children playing under Marianna's supervision as if they were friends of long standing. '*Buona sera, Mama,* Nell.' He didn't wait; he jumped straight in. 'I had an idea…'

'Really, *bello*?'

'No need to make it sound such a landmark, Mother.'

The shrewd blue gaze remained on his face, prompting him to say what he had on his mind. 'It's impossibly hot in the city. The scheme is running smoothly. I thought we should all take off, and go up to the chalet.'

'To the chalet?' The *contessa* thought about it. 'That *is* a good idea, *bello*. But don't you have work to do?'

'I couldn't possibly leave,' Nell confirmed, shaking her head.

Luca had anticipated that. 'This is the ideal opportunity for you to see if your scheme works without you, Nell. Or aren't you ready to test it yet?' He knew she couldn't resist the challenge.

'I'm ready to stand in for you, Nell,' his mother cut in, as he had also anticipated. 'But who will take your place, Luca?' She shook her head, but more to give him an opening than to point up any problems with his idea, Luca suspected.

'I have a full team at the moment. They can do without me for a couple of days.'

'You not suggesting we go away together?' Nell looked horrified at the prospect.

He fielded both women at once. 'I'm covered at the hospital, and we'll take the children with us. I'm suggesting a long weekend of mountain air, Nell, not a prolonged sojourn in my harem.'

'Luca!' His mother frowned severely at him. Then their gazes locked and understanding dawned in her eyes. 'The children love it here. Why do you want to disturb them?' She turned to Nell. 'The heat doesn't affect them at all, does it?'

'But surely the heat affects you, Contessa?' Nell said. 'You'd like to go to the mountains, wouldn't you?'

'I won't be hot in Venice if I'm taking over from you in an air-conditioned hospital,' the *contessa* pointed out. 'And Marianna won't leave the children…'

'So you and I will take off, Nell,' Luca finished.

Nell gasped, but his mother only managed to spear him a look as if to say she was surprised any son of hers had taken so long coming to the point. But then she didn't appreciate the subtlety required. He'd tried the way that came naturally to him and found he'd made no progress at all—and normally, whenever a door slammed in his face he could usually find a window to climb through…

But as he eased the collar of his shirt Luca wondered if he might self-combust before Nell gave him her answer. Taking things at such a slow pace was not his *modus operandi* of choice.

Before Nell had chance to get over her shock at his suggestion, his mother held up her hand. She was wearing the mock-innocent expression she always employed whenever she was on the verge of pulling off some great coup. 'But going up to the chalet is a wonderful idea! Didn't I say you should spoil yourself a little, Nell?'

'I'm not sure...' Nell's brow puckered up.

He could see she was thrown by the fact that his mother was all for his suggestion. Having the *contessa*'s endorsement gave it a seal of respectability, of propriety...

'You'll be all the better for coming fresh to your work, Nell,' his mother added. 'But of course, it's up to you. I wouldn't dream of influencing you.' Closing her eyes, she sank back in her seat.

When the devil came tempting, he didn't wear Chanel and have centuries of refinement and good sense to back him up, Nell thought as she stared at the *contessa*. All she really wanted was someone to push her over the line between, 'No, I couldn't possibly,' and, 'Why not?' And the *contessa* was a good friend, someone she had come to trust in the short time she'd known her.

'You know what Molly will say, don't you?' Lifting her head, the *contessa* smiled at Nell.

As a family the Barbaros had perfected the art of the low blow. Molly frequently complained to Nell that she should give her some space. It was a typical pre-teen moan, but it wouldn't have surprised Nell to learn that Molly had confided all the details of their latest minor disagreement to the *contessa*.

'It's not forever,' the *contessa* cajoled.

'Just a long weekend,' Luca added.

'And the air in the mountains would do you so much good.'

'What do you think?'

As Nell held Luca's stare she had to stifle the buzz of excitement she felt in case it showed in her eyes. 'We wouldn't be alone?'

'Alone?' the *contessa* exclaimed. 'Certainly not. We keep a large staff at the chalet. There isn't a chance of you being alone. Do you think I would expose you to gossip, Nell?' She opened her eyes very wide.

But that was a hard one. Something told Nell the *contessa* would be totally indifferent to gossip.

Luca was beginning to show all the signs of a man who had been forced to sit down too long. If anything, he looked bored by the whole discussion, Nell thought, watching him ease his powerful legs as he stood up.

'Too many women for you, *bello*?' his mother teased, seeing Molly come running up to them.

'I've always got time for this one.' His brooding mood changed in an instant. Catching Molly to him, he swung her high into the air, and as she heard her daughter's delighted squeal, Nell realised she had made a decision.

CHAPTER TWELVE

THE large staff turned out to be one smiling cook and her husband, who told Nell in perfect English that he was gardener-cum-snow-shoveller, as well as general factotum to Luca's family when they were in residence. And he couldn't have been happier to welcome her to the *palazzo*.

'*Palazzo?*' Nell murmured, gazing at Luca. 'Another one?'

'An affectation of the staff. I think of it as a chalet.' His lips pressed down as he shrugged.

'You seem blessed with an overabundance of very large houses. And talking of the large staff your mother referred to, where are they?'

'It's late summer—they must be away on holiday.'

'All of them?' If such a large force ever existed at all, Nell thought, realising they were probably going to be left pretty much to their own devices. When Luca had spoken about a chalet, Nell had pictured something small and quaint such as she had seen in Switzerland, but the word *palazzo* put everything in its proper perspective. Chalet Aquila was only quaint as far as its wooden walls and steeply pitched ceilings were concerned. Small, it was not. But there was a benefit to that, Nell reassured herself. She could easily find her own private space in the library, or the snug, or even outside on the fabulous, glass-lined balcony overlooking the mountains.

Perhaps the *contessa* was right after all, Nell decided as she started to unpack in her room. This break in the mountains was just what she needed.

'Dinner at eight?'

Her feet almost left the ground as Luca poked his head round the door. Their bedrooms were on separate wings, which had reassured her, but she hadn't expected things to be so casual.

'Sorry…should have knocked,' he said.

'Yes, you should!'

He found it hard to hold back, hard to adjust to all the strictures he'd placed upon himself now that he had decided to woo Nell properly. But, seeing her expression when he took her by surprise, he gathered that his new career as her respectful suitor would be short-lived if he couldn't adapt. What he wanted to do was walk right in and take her on the bed. It was about time. But no…he had to hold himself in check and curb his natural instincts—adopt the sex-drive of a sloth.

'I'll see you at dinner,' she said firmly.

'I thought I'd take a walk first.' Maybe the crisp night air might cool his ardour! 'If you need anything, just ask Maria or Tomas.'

So she was to be left alone. Was Luca regretting his invitation already? Nell stood motionless, listening to Luca's footsteps disappearing down the wooden steps until he reached the ground floor. Then she hurried across to the window overlooking the front of the house, where she could see the path leading from the front door. Why hadn't he invited her along? She would have liked a walk…

She had never taken such trouble with her appearance, Nell realised. She was doing it out of pique because Luca was making it clear he wasn't interested and she had no intention of losing her self-esteem. No woman, however determined she was to resist a man, liked to think she was invisible.

She was glad Molly had talked her into packing a floaty dress. The shops in Venice were irresistible and this was one crazy purchase she would almost certainly never wear again. Gossamer-fine and very feminine, it weighed almost nothing. And it came out of her overnight bag without so much as a crease.

Nell's heart started thundering the moment she walked through the door to join him for dinner. Luca had made less of an effort, but then he always looked stunning even in jeans. They clung snugly to his lean hips and the chunky belt drew attention to his firm torso. There was just enough bronze to tempt her gaze beneath the open buttons of his black linen shirt, and she had a thing for powerful forearms, especially when, like Luca's, they were shaded with dark hair. His feet were bare, which for some reason she found extremely sexy.

And this was dinner with a colleague?

Yes, and if she didn't know the difference between that and a date, it was time for a reality check. But his hair was still damp from the shower and he smelled great as he held her chair. Full marks for being a gentleman in the dining room; nil for his manners in the bedroom.

A smiling Maria served them a delicious meal. Nell tried out her Italian, and was pleased to find herself understood. She was picking it up almost as quickly as Molly. Luca made no comment, not even when she glanced at him as Maria praised her efforts. He was more sphinx-like than the sphinx, except when she turned the conversation to her scheme—only then did he become animated. On the whole, though, their conversation seemed more of a chore than a pleasure.

She was disappointed, but not surprised, when he stood up the moment they had finished coffee.

'Well, I think I'm going to get an early night.'

'You're going to bed now?' She stared at him.

'The mountain air.' He stifled a yawn. 'I hope you will excuse me.'

Was she boring him? 'Of course.'

As the door shut Nell threw herself back in her chair. Luca wiped out by the altitude—Luca, who never tired? She wasn't affected at all! But then he had been out for a walk…perhaps he had taken one of the mountain lifts in the area. That must be it, because surely it wasn't high enough here for the altitude to affect him? And she certainly wasn't ready for bed yet. She had far too much energy—and nothing to expend it on.

Maria pointed Nell in the direction of a gym in the basement, where she worked out, and then took a sauna. After showering, she dressed in the towelling robe she found in the communal bathroom off the gym. Collecting a mug of hot chocolate from the kitchen, she wandered into the snug to take in a film. It was well past midnight by the time she climbed the stairs.

Hesitating on the landing to check everyone was asleep, Nell couldn't help peering down the corridor towards the bedroom where Luca was sleeping. There wasn't a sound to be heard, and all the doors were firmly closed.

Retiring to her own room, she went inside and shut the door. Then she opened it again—just a crack. Then a little bit more. Perhaps Luca would want to check up on her, to make sure she was all right?

Or not.

Either way, she didn't want to lock herself away like Rapunzel in the tower.

The night was long and Nell heard every creak and

grumble as the warm timbers cooled. But unfortunately, none of those noises heralded Luca creeping down the corridor towards her room.

Not that she wanted him to, of course.

At breakfast the next morning she was red-eyed and irritable.

'Sleep well?' Luca enquired brightly, appearing not to notice how she looked or what mood she was in. 'The bed wasn't lumpy, was it?' he pressed when she didn't answer.

No; in fact, the bed had been perfect. Wide, firm, cosy… and decidedly empty, as he very well knew. Which was just as it should be. Nell ground her jaw as she made slow progress along the delicious buffet Maria had set out for them.

'You seem…'

'Yes?' she demanded snappily, rounding on Luca.

'Oh, I don't know. Edgy?'

'Must be the altitude getting to me. Only it's having the opposite effect on me. All you want to do is sleep, while I…'

'Yes?'

She wasn't going to admit that he was the cause of her restless night. 'Well, it's a strange bed. I can never sleep on the first night.'

'Really?' He appeared to think about it. 'Shall we eat outside? The fresh air will do you good.'

Nell hummed sceptically.

'Or perhaps I could recommend something to help you sleep?'

'No, thank you. I'll be all right.'

'I mean, like a bracing walk,' he clarified.

'To tire me out?' There was a band of tension stretching between them that only the most strenuous of walks could possibly alleviate.

'Exactly.'

Although perhaps that band of tension was all on her side.

Luca seemed perfectly relaxed, which had the effect of making Nell even more strung out. 'Good idea,' she said without much enthusiasm. Sitting down, she forced herself to eat.

But the picnic in the mountains exceeded all Nell's expectations. Luca urged her on until they reached a meadow carpeted with wild flowers. Apart from the beauty surrounding her, which was certainly a distraction, there was no problem with her carnal urges—they were well and truly subdued after the demanding trek.

'You'll sleep well tonight,' Luca observed with a maddening degree of confidence.

'I certainly will,' Nell said, playing his game as she flopped onto the ground with relief. Rolling onto her stomach, she lifted herself up on her elbows to look beyond the plateau they had reached to the view beyond. The snow-capped mountains formed a crescent around the lush green valley far below them. Dragging her gaze away, she ran her fingers through the mass of flowers that seemed to proliferate where they had set up camp. 'I never imagined there would be so many flowers this late in the summer. And the air's so fresh.'

'The altitude,' Luca reminded her. 'We're high above the pollution from the city here. And plants at this height keep on flowering until the first snows, and even then they peep through until they're completely buried.'

They sat together on a blanket Luca had brought in a roll on top of the rucksack containing their food. It wasn't a large rug, and once the food was laid out on it and they were sitting down it was almost impossible to keep a space between them.

Nell held herself aloof, but she noticed that Luca seemed to be a different man in the mountains. He was relaxed and totally at ease with the silence, as if the cool, clean air had gently lifted the stresses of his demanding work from his face.

'What a contrast it is here to Venice,' she observed. 'And yet we're so close.'

'When the skies are clear it's sometimes possible to see these mountains from the city, but it's been too muggy recently.'

'But lovely all the same. You're so lucky to have two of the most beautiful places in the world at your disposal.'

'Yes, I am,' he agreed without pretence that it might be otherwise.

As he gazed out across the valley in silence, Nell's imagination took flight. This was the perfect moment, the moment in which the hero in any novel might reach across and kiss her. As Luca turned to face her their eyes locked and the breath caught in her throat...

'Turkey or ham?'

'I beg your pardon?' Nell blinked at him.

'Turkey or ham?' he repeated. He was holding a panini in each hand, offering her the choice.

They munched along in silence, drinking fresh raspberry juice, which was delicious. But, while nothing could have been improved upon and she had no complaints, Nell still felt dissatisfied. She might be determined to resist the attraction between them, but she didn't want to be ignored by Luca either!

'You look tired,' he observed with approval as they started collecting up the picnic things. 'This should help you sleep tonight.'

'Yes. Thank you.' Keeping her features composed, Nell dipped her head and concentrated on the rug she was folding.

She buried her head beneath the pillows and tried to turn her mind to something else. But that wasn't easy when Luca was sleeping in a room just a short walk away.

It was three o'clock in the morning and she was wide awake. Sitting up in bed, she rubbed her eyes and checked the clock on the mantelpiece. She slid her legs over the side of the bed, padded to the door and opened it a crack.

Silence greeted her. Deciding to get a drink, she crept downstairs in the dark, not wanting to put a light on and cause concern. Opening the kitchen the door very carefully so it didn't squeak, she walked inside.

'Luca!' She took a pace back. 'What are you doing here?'

'I might ask you the same question. I couldn't sleep.'

'So the picnic didn't work?'

'For you either.' His lips tugged down in wry amusement.

'Must be the altitude.'

'Must be.'

There was an edge of irony in his voice. 'Camomile tea?' she suggested lightly, spotting various herbal infusions on a shelf.

Luca tipped his whisky glass towards her. 'Can I tempt you to something stronger?'

'No, I don't think so.' Temptation was behind them, where she intended it to stay.

Two minutes later, the tension humming through her body, the awareness twanging her nerves, Nell was wondering why on earth she hadn't grabbed a cold drink and fled instead of putting the kettle on. But she was quite safe, she reminded herself—wild hair, no make-up and comfy men's pyjamas from a market stall hardly made it look as though she was attempting to seduce him!

The drink was ready at last. 'I'm off to bed, then,' she mumbled.

Luca gave her a fast glance. Was he imagining it, or had she been dawdling? 'Goodnight.' He kept the voice clipped, impersonal, but he didn't start breathing properly again until he heard her bedroom door close a few minutes later.

If this was what it meant to behave with propriety, to

court a woman properly, to turn Nell from rejecting him because she thought he only wanted sex into pursuing him because he showed no interest, he could only hope she had an epiphany soon—like right away, before the frustration made something explode.

He'd done with wooing like a sloth, Luca decided the next morning. He'd had no sleep at all and it clearly wasn't working. Some things just weren't meant to be. He'd have breakfast first and then go where his instinct was telling him to go, do what he had to do...

He followed the delicious aroma of coffee, toast and freshly scrambled egg into the kitchen, then pulled up short when he saw who was cooking. 'Where's Maria?'

'It's her day off, isn't it?' Nell pointed out.

She didn't look up from the eggs she was stirring in the skillet and her hair had fallen forward over her face so all that he could see was a fine trace of pale silhouette edging a dark cloud of silky hair. He wanted to run his hands through it, over it and then down the expanse of naked neck showing above the simple top she was wearing. Then he would transfer his attention to her breasts before licking his way down to her navel...

'Soft, moist and runny, or dry?'

He stared at her, speechless.

'Eggs,' she elucidated. 'Scrambled eggs. Some people can't bear them sloppy. I prefer them that way myself.'

'Right. Yes. Me too. You didn't have to make breakfast, but I'm glad you did.' He let the smile back into his voice. 'Maria would have been only too happy to make something before she left, though.'

'I didn't think it was fair to keep her on her day off. I'm quite capable of scrambling an egg.'

'I'm sure you are.' He wasn't even aware that his voice had faded as they stared at each other.

'Taste?' She held out the wooden spoon.

He hesitated, not trusting himself to behave.

'People like different amounts of seasoning. I wasn't sure…' Now it was the turn of Nell's voice to dwindle. 'Luca, what's the matter? Don't you feel well? I know you couldn't sleep last night, but…'

'I've never felt better,' he said honestly, watching her blue eyes darken. But he wanted more than a quick coupling…a lot more. The sexual charge between them was always there, but he was greedy for more now. He wanted to connect, to belong, to share, to open up… He wanted so many things that he had never wanted before, and had never had the opportunity to claim for himself.

'Mustn't let the eggs spoil.' She turned back to the cooker, clearly flustered by what she could see in his face.

'More toast?' she murmured later as he was tucking into a second helping.

Damn, she was a good cook. 'Mmm,' he said, wiping his lips on a napkin. He stood up to save her crossing the kitchen with the fresh slices. When she passed him the plate the toast slipped, and as they both dived to save it somehow they became entangled. His hand moved up her arm to her breast—

'No, Luca!' Freeing herself, she held up her hands as if to ward him off. 'We came here for a rest.'

'You came here to be with me,' he told her, sure of his ground.

She raked her hair in a gesture he recognised from years back. 'That isn't fair. You're not fair!'

'What? Telling the truth isn't fair?'

'Oh, it's so easy for you, isn't it? But I know it's all an act!'

'An *act*? What act?' Suddenly he was shouting too. And then she was tangled in his arms again, half-kissing, half-fighting. But even then she managed to surprise him. Reaching up, she laced her fingers through his hair in an attempt to drag him down to her.

'No, Nell!' He pulled back.

'*No?*' The black passion in her eyes turned to blue ice.

'No. We've tried that already and we know it doesn't work.' His voice was steady, reasoned, but he could see twin spots of fury forming on her cheeks. It was always like that between them, passion so close to the surface it only took the slightest encouragement to break free.

'What, then?' Her voice was anguished as she turned her face up to him. He knew it reflected all the hurt and anger she felt inside. 'How should we behave towards each other, Luca?'

He held her firmly when she tried to break away. 'I'll tell you how, and it isn't like this. I don't want to have sex with you. I want to make love to you—and there's one hell of a difference.'

His words hung in the air between them as if they both needed time to absorb what he'd said.

'Luca…'

Cupping her chin, he made sure of her silence the only way he knew how. When he let her go again she stood breathless, staring up at him.

She had no idea that he could be so tender, or that a kiss started in passion could turn into music that sang in her soul, tuning her body to his so acutely she knew they were one.

He nuzzled her face again, rough stubble against soft skin. Closing her eyes, she let her lips part and gasped to feel his tongue. He was teasing her, withdrawing before she had time to get used to the sensation, then capturing the full swell of her bottom lip, tugging gently, so gently he almost made her cry. It raised every tiny hair on the back of her neck, and as her limbs softened with desire his arms went around her and he lifted her, carrying her across the room towards the door…

Luca's bedroom was almost identical to her own. Shady and cool, with linen blinds drawn low across the picture windows. Beyond them the windows must have been open because the cream shades were billowing lightly in the stiff morning breeze.

She shivered as he set her down.

'You're not cold, are you?'

'I think we both know I'm not.'

Luca's eyes were slumberous, hiding his expression. 'I suppose I should know everything about you, since I'm a doctor. And it's not like me to misdiagnose.'

'There's always a first time, Doctor.' Humour had always been a cover for their insecurities and awkwardness. Now, suddenly, it had become something more, a secret connection that was a symbol of the journey they had taken together.

'I'd better check I can still remember where all your pleasure zones are located. It's been so long I may have forgotten what to do.'

'I doubt it,' Nell murmured, sinking lower on the bed as Luca lay down beside her, 'but if you have forgotten, after my experience at the carnival I should be able to talk you through it.'

'I can't wait.' He smiled as he dropped a kiss on her brow, on her eyelids, on her mouth…

He was so gentle with her, his fingers light as he tucked a strand of hair behind her ear. His hands moved over her, sending tiny darts of pleasure coursing through her. She was on fire for him. She wanted everything he could give her…but she wanted his kisses most of all.

Tilting her chin, he stared into her eyes. 'You frighten me,' he whispered.

And then she didn't have chance to question him because his lips claimed hers, his tongue probing, seeking, while his hands showed all the longing she dared hope for.

'I frighten *you*?' she murmured later, searching his gaze. 'I've never felt like this before…'

'Then that's good,' Luca whispered against her mouth, 'because it wouldn't be fair for only one of us to suffer.' Tracing the length of her arm with one fingertip, he finally took her hand and laced their fingers together. 'I want this to last, Nell.'

'For how long?' she whispered.

'Forever.'

'Forever?'

But he silenced her with another kiss, and then, brushing his chin against her face, he made her whimper. She could feel his warmth and his strength in every fibre of her being. 'It's like the first time…' Turning her face up, she stared deep into his eyes. 'I want you, Luca.'

'I think I know that.' He smiled as he kicked off his shoes, and then, removing her sandals, began caressing her feet, manipulating them skilfully.

She moaned softly. 'I didn't even know I liked this…'

'Then you have everything to discover.'

He caressed her breasts, pushing her top out of the way so he could move on to her belly, where he teased her by running his fingers beneath the waistband of her jeans. He brushed her lightly between her legs to hear her moan. He could feel her heat, sense her need… Her lips were slightly parted and as he teased her some more she eased her legs apart, inviting more. Reluctantly, he refused the offer. It was far too soon.

Her pulse leapt when he eased her top over her head and she was already loosening her jeans. He put his hands over hers, stopping her. There was a long way to go before she was ready for that.

'Why?'

He moved down the bed as she spoke, laving kisses on her

breasts, on her belly, licking, nipping, preparing her. 'Because I'm not ready yet.'

Her eyes called him a liar, and unfortunately it was true. He was at crisis point, thrusting hard against the opening of his jeans. But he could hold back, and so she would too.

He ripped off his shirt in one impatient movement, exulting when Nell's hands went immediately to press against his chest.

'You're so hard...you're magnificent.'

Taking hold of her hands, he kissed each one of her fingertips in turn. 'And you're beautiful...the most beautiful woman I've ever known.' They had both waited so long for this trial of sensual endurance, he wouldn't spoil it now by allowing the heat building up inside him to take over. He wanted tenderness and sensuality for both of them, and he would have it, even though her eyes were entreating him, her lips begging him...

She nearly destroyed his self-will when she nipped each of his hard brown nipples in turn between her thumb and forefinger. And then she writhed against him and he had to grit his teeth and think of everything but how much he wanted her. But even then he just grew harder. Her voice was a seduction, her body a sin... He found the answer in lifting himself out of real time so that he could observe her clinically, telling himself in a mind- if not body-numbing mantra how much better he could make it for her if only she would wait. But how he wanted to express all the feeling welling inside him: caring, cherishing, loving...

'Kiss me, Luca.'

He needed no encouragement. Cupping her face in his hands, he kissed her deeply. All the barriers between them broke down and disappeared as he prolonged the kiss, stroking her tongue, sucking it, plundering, moving and thrusting in a shadow of the act she craved so desperately. He moved to her breasts, capturing first one nipple and then the other, heating them with his hot breath until they strained towards him, begging to be sucked, flaunting themselves through a tormenting barrier of flimsy lace.

He refused to be hurried, and only smiled when she called out to him to try and urge him on. He lingered at the waistband of her briefs, and just when he knew she couldn't stand any more he moved down the bed again and started massaging her feet.

She was so frustrated she tried to roll away, but he caught her to him easily. He was still laughing softly when he started licking behind her knees, and thrilled to realise that she'd had no idea she was so sensitive there. How little she knew of love. Reaching up his hands, he began to stroke her thighs, tantalising her by sweeping short of where she needed him to be. He could feel her quivering. Moving up the bed, he let her feel his weight, just for a moment, his hard, toned frame pressing into her. Then, slipping his hand beneath her briefs, he stroked her belly, reaching down to feather a torment between her legs...stretching delicately, tugging a little, then stroking, but always missing the special place where she longed for his attention. She kept adjusting her position in an attempt to outwit him, but he kept her still with one hand while with two fingers of the other hand he began to massage gently.

'Now, now,' she begged hoarsely, as once again he avoided touching her most sensitive place.

She was trembling all over, shaking so much she could hardly speak. His answer was to dip his tongue into the hollow at the base of her neck and lick her until she begged for mercy, and only then did he lower the straps of her bra.

'I hate you!' she told him softly when he looked up.

'I know. But not for long.'

He weighed her breasts appreciatively as a prelude to

laving them with his tongue. Her nipples strained towards him, and her smooth, pale skin was flushed rose-pink after he had rasped his beard against her. Now she was arching against him, calling out for release.

'Do you still hate me?' he teased. 'Because if you want more you must lie still and be a good girl…' He gazed down, frowning, pretending disapproval, as she thrust her hips towards him. 'What are you doing?'

The stern tone of his voice made her tremble even more. What did she have to do? 'You're impossible!' she accused him.

The result of his teasing was clearly defined beneath the cobweb fabric of her briefs; the tone of his voice had aroused her all the more. 'Please, Luca, no more teasing. I can't bear this… You're…' Her voice faded into a groan as he touched her lightly between the legs. Drawing her knees back, she writhed beneath him.

'Impossible?' he supplied drily.

'Worse than that…' was all she could manage. She was sobbing with frustration. As he cupped her buttocks she exhaled raggedly.

'You greedy girl,' he murmured. 'Can't you wait?'

'No!'

'Well, you won't be needing these.' Catching hold of the waistband of her briefs, he slipped them off.

Her eyes slanted like a cat's as she smiled her satisfaction. 'Now,' she commanded in a whisper.

'Maybe I don't think you're ready yet—' He gasped, the words stolen from his lips as she took him firmly in her hands.

'I think I am,' she said, wrapping her legs around his waist.

CHAPTER THIRTEEN

SHE might be acting strong, but he was going to take precautions first and then she could do what she liked with him.

He eased into her, taking care not to hurt her. There was something different between them now, something that demanded all his attention.

'Wait,' she said abruptly.

He stopped immediately when she asked him to. She didn't speak; he just felt her hands pressing against his chest. 'Am I hurting you?'

She was panting, tensing, Nell realised. The size of him… how had she forgotten? It had always been fast, animalistic, almost feral before, like two wild beasts without thought or care. But this was different in every way, tender, exquisitely sensitive. Nothing could have prepared her…

'No… I don't want you to stop. It's like the first time…'

'For me too.'

He kissed her deeply, caressing her at the same time, finding her and stroking her while he drove steadily on. His touch was so persuasive, so delicate and intuitive. He waited until she had relaxed completely, and then it was she who made the first move, lifting her hips towards him so that he could inhabit her completely.

His warm breath raced against her ear, delivering tiny electric shocks throughout her system. She held his gaze, tightening her muscles around him and working her hips so that he was rubbing rhythmically against her, yet making no attempt to withdraw...

Without warning, she came violently, clinging to him, crying, bucking, gasping, greedily working her body against his to make it last.

He made it last.

Luca understood every part of her. He knew how to prolong the pleasure and how to gently persuade her she wanted more. 'I'm not ready... I can't be...'

But he was right. Her innermost muscles were already clenching and relaxing in anticipation as she writhed provocatively beneath him. He took her again, plunging deep, working steadily, only pausing each time she climaxed.

Maybe he had made her wait too long. She was so frustrated, it was like having to skim the cream off the top of the milk before you could drink it. She was completely abandoned, lying with her knees back, opening herself for him, every inhibition lost in the frantic hunt for pleasure. His muscles were hard and bunched beneath her hands where she had grabbed his hips to urge him on.

The light was fading by the time he released her, and only then did he wonder about the desperation he'd sensed in her as they made love. Was she still so unsure of him?

It was their last night at Chalet Aquila and yet it was their first real night together. Had she become an addiction he couldn't break? Luca wondered as he soothed Nell with kisses. He had never expected it to be like this when he had taken time to make it special for her. He had never expected her to be so vulnerable. But when she had turned to him with her eyes wide and frightened when he was making love to her, it was almost as if she was anticipating rejection…rejection at the very moment when he had cherished her the most.

Who had done this to her? Who had hurt her? It had to be Molly's father. Jake.

Tipping up her chin so he could look into her eyes, he saw the deep-rooted fear she always tried so hard to hide, and knew then there was still so much she wasn't telling him. 'Nell…don't hold out on me.'

'Hold out on you?'

She tried the smile, the confident, sensuous curve of her lips that at one time would have been enough for him to forget any question he might have had in mind, but not this time. 'Nell…' His look told her he was prepared to wait for however long it took.

Her smile faded, her eyes flickered and then she turned her head away. Cupping her chin, he gently brought her back again. Why was she still keeping secrets from him? What did he have to do to prove himself to her? Weren't they close enough yet? Didn't she know he would never hurt her intentionally? The last thing on earth he wanted to do was to turn her back into the hostile individual he had first encountered on the banks of the canal. His only thought now was to protect her. 'You demand honesty of me,' he said gently.

'Yes,' she said, meeting his gaze.

'Then why can't you be honest with me?'

'I am honest with you,' she protested.

'So, tell me about Jake.'

She froze in his arms. 'What do you want to know?' Sitting up, she bunched her knees under her chin and wrapped her arms around them.

'Everything.'

'I already told you why I couldn't trust doctors.' She

stopped and glanced up at the ceiling as if she was struggling to hold in her feelings.

'But there's more to it than that, isn't there, Nell? It wasn't just me as a doctor you were hostile towards when we first met. There was a barricade around you a mile wide.'

'When we first met I had a sick child, and you were Molly's doctor. Do you really think that would have been a good time to start an affair with you?'

'I'm not talking about starting an affair. I'm only interested in the defences you had in place—and why they were there. You still had them when I saw you speaking on the platform in that suit—'

'So, you're judging me on my clothes?'

'Your armour,' he argued softly.

He was right, but it had been a long fight back after Jake's deception. She couldn't forget how that lack of judgement had torn her world apart. With sex and men out of the picture she had felt safe, but now she was vulnerable again. And there was Molly to consider. Could she pretend not to have noticed how Molly's face lit up every time Luca was around? Could she take the risk that, if things went further, he might let them down as Jake had done?

She took a breath. 'I was married—I thought happily. I was pregnant with my first child. We had everything to live for. Then a policewoman came to the door one day. She said, "There's been an accident…"'

It was as if the colour surrounding her had abruptly turned to black and white. As she told him about her husband's fatal accident, he understood what had hurt her even more than the sense of helplessness. She had been betrayed. He listened as she told him about the other woman, the woman who had held Jake's baby in her arms. She couldn't hate that woman, or her baby, and then he knew that Nell had turned that hatred on herself. She didn't need to tell him how much it hurt, because he could feel it for her.

'I didn't know what to do,' she whispered.

No. She had been vulnerable and alone. And that was why when he met her all those years ago in Venice she had been so angry and frightened. She had believed she was to blame again, but this time for Molly's illness.

'But why do you still feel guilty?' he prompted gently.

She didn't speak for a while and then she tipped her chin up to face him. 'Because everything that happened came from me wanting something I couldn't have. Jake was so wild, so exciting, and I was…'

'What?'

'Can't you see?'

'No, I can't see.' A sudden surge of anger blinded him. He was angry with himself, with Nell. What was she trying to say? Did she still love her dead husband?

'I wasn't enough for Jake,' she said starkly. 'That was why he needed someone else. It hurt to find that out. And if I'm still hiding behind those defences you were talking about, it's because I don't want to be hurt again.'

'You don't need to hide to achieve that. You simply need to know your lover would not betray you.'

She didn't respond to that, staring at her hands, and Luca felt a wave of sheer, painful rage as he realised what her silence meant.

'So you think all men are the same as Jake? That we would all break our vows so lightly?'

She hesitated too long. 'Thank you,' he said tensely.

'Thank you for what?' She glanced at him warily.

'You're too fond of pigeon-holing people, Nell. Doctors, nurses, men in general, Latin men in particular…all of us neatly labelled and filed away in your head.' Holding her gaze firm, he saw he was right. He swung out of bed and started throwing on his clothes. 'Do you have any more insults up your sleeve? Please, don't hold back—or shall I try to guess? The Latin lover who lies and cheats his way through countless women? Is that it, Nell? Do you really think you can tar me with the same brush as Jake?'

'No, of course not—'

'Then what?'

She didn't know. All she could hold on to was the knowledge that it was she who was inadequate. Why else had Jake made a parallel life with another woman? She couldn't risk that happening a second time, not with Molly to consider.

'Jake was a weakling, a coward. I hope you're not suggesting I am too?'

She flinched from Luca's tightly controlled anger, but she also felt a shock of surprise. 'A coward?' She had always seen Jake as a man who sparkled brighter than a diamond. And Luca was so far from being a coward, his suggestion was risible.

'Yes, a coward,' he repeated scathingly. 'What else would you call a man who refuses to live up to his responsibilities, a man who cannot face the woman he married and tell her the truth, a man who lied to two women, both of them bearing his child. Contemptible.' With a sound of disgust, he shook his head.

Nell opened her mouth to protest, and shut it again. She had simply never looked at it from that point of view, but suddenly she found it hard to believe that she had shut her mind to Jake's responsibility for so long.

'But surely it must have been hard for him. With two women, two children…' She hardly realised she was speaking out loud. She was still trying to make sense of it, trying to look back at her marriage from the new perspective Luca had just given her.

'Are you making excuses for him?'

'No, of course not.' It had been an automatic response, after years trapped in the web of self-delusion that insisted *she* was to blame for the breakdown of her marriage.

Luca was staring at her incredulously. 'I don't believe you.'

'Luca, don't look at me like that—'

'Do you still love him?'

'What?'

'Do you still love him?'

Loving Jake was so far from her mind, Nell's brain locked. Nothing would come to her lips. She held out her hand as Luca started for the door.

'Perhaps it's as well our time in the mountains is almost at an end,' he snapped at her. 'I'll leave you to shower. Use my bathroom and then go and pack.'

'Pack?'

'There's no reason why we shouldn't go back to Venice this evening. I don't see any point in staying here now. As far as I'm concerned we might as well leave right away, in fact.' His voice was so cold, so hard.

Nell's head was reeling. She couldn't believe Luca thought she still loved Jake, but in this mood he wouldn't listen whatever she said. She tried anyway as he stalked away. 'Luca, it's not that I love Jake—'

He paused at the door. 'Do you really think you have the monopoly on feelings?'

'No, of course not. Luca, please listen—'

With a contemptuous sound he walked out of the room, slamming the door behind him as if he couldn't wait to put distance between them.

If she had thought the drive back to Venice in total silence was hard, the arrival was much worse. Molly's crestfallen face when Nell arrived back early said it all. But what had she thought her reception would be like, when she had returned to the *palazzo* with red-rimmed eyes and Luca was so tense he could barely speak to anyone?

What had she allowed Molly to think? Nell felt a shaft of guilt pierce her as she met her daughter's anxious, enquiring gaze. That there was a romance brewing between her mother and a man Molly clearly adored? If she had done that, it wasn't merely careless, it was unforgivable.

'Well, you can go back to the hotel if you like, but I'm not coming with you,' Molly announced mulishly.

'What?' Nell refocused. 'Oh, yes, you are, young lady. It's time for bed.'

'In my pyjamas?' Molly held out the sides of her baggy trousers. 'You said you'd be back on Monday, so I got changed ready for bed.'

'Well, you can get changed back again.'

'I don't want to!'

'Don't worry, Molly, you can stay over on another occasion.'

Nell and Molly turned to stare at Luca, with very different expressions on their faces.

Having Luca side with her threw Nell for a moment. She was torn between holding firm and being reasonable. Just because her weekend had finished so very badly was no reason to ruin Molly's.

She sighed. 'If the *contessa* doesn't mind you staying over—' She hardly got the words out before Molly whooped with joy, threw her arms around her neck and kissed her roundly on the cheek and then skipped off.

Before her mother had a chance to change her mind, Nell thought wryly, watching her.

'The boat's right outside,' Luca said coolly.

'Oh, no, thank you. But if you'd like to call a taxi—'

'That will take longer.'

And he couldn't bear her there a moment longer than necessary. 'If you're sure it's no trouble?'

'None at all.'

Luca dropped Nell off at the landing stage outside her hotel. In the time it took them to cross the canal neither of them spoke a word. As she disembarked outside the hotel, Nell thanked him and then paused only to confirm their plans.

'There's no reason to change the time of our meeting, is there?' he asked abruptly.

'Well, no, of course not, but—'

'Then goodnight.'

He was already turning the boat around, watching the sides didn't scrape against the wharf, visually measuring the space in which he had to turn the prow without banging into any of the mooring posts. Dismissing her.

'Goodnight, Luca,' she whispered. 'And thank you again.'

For the weekend? For the boat trip back to her hotel? He didn't know, and right now he didn't care. He had fallen in love with a woman who was still in love with her dead husband, even if Nell might not know it herself. Better to face up to the truth now than to run away from it, as she had been. Firming his jaw, Luca opened up the throttle and turned the boat for home.

The next day Nell found herself staring at Luca's empty chair and thinking it a symbol for their relationship. She had arrived early for their meeting after a sleepless night, and had begun by making a few phone calls. The rest of the time she had spent sorting through the things she would take with her without actually seeing any of them. She was still numb after Luca's accusation that she loved Jake. The dismay she felt was not just at the inaccuracy of his assertion but at the discovery that Luca was as vulnerable as she was. And she hadn't reached out to him once.

They'd had one night untainted by the past, and that, ironically, had been the night of the carnival, when they had each taken refuge in the past. Hiding behind masks had allowed them to meet and fall in love as if they were strangers. It was all so clear now. But the moment reality had broken through again, neither of them had been able to change who they were...at least, not enough.

But still they'd stumbled on, adding one building block at a time to the knowledge and understanding they'd gained of each other, and it hurt to think that they had parted so bitterly at a time when they had never been closer. But then the only thing that had always eluded them was trust...

And now it was too late to mend the rift.

Hearing footsteps, Nell pulled herself together. She had the volunteers to think about. She had to make sure that everything was in order for them before she left.

Luca swept in with the briefest of greetings, sat down, pulled out a sheaf of documents from his briefcase, and scanned them briefly. 'There's not much left for you to do here, is there?'

'That's right.' Was he relieved? Her leaving would certainly put an end to the disruption she had brought to his perfectly ordered life.

'So, you'll be moving on again?'

'I'll be returning home with Molly and Marianna.'

'And when will that be?'

'As soon as I can confirm the flights.' That wasn't true. She had already confirmed the flights while she had been waiting for him. They would be leaving tomorrow, since there was no reason for her to stay in Venice. She dreaded telling Molly, but it would only get harder the longer they stayed.

'Do you need any help with that? I know people at the airport.'

And have him know what her plans were? Better to make a clean break. 'No, thank you. It's all in hand.'

'So it's all over?'

'All over?' Nell repeated, following Molly's gaze out of the aircraft window. They were a few minutes into the flight and the plane was banking steeply as it made a turn to climb above the mountains she had visited with Luca.

'You know what I mean.' Molly's voice was tight, and she wouldn't meet her gaze.

Nell glanced round at Marianna, but she was fast asleep. 'Darling, I'm—'

'What?' Molly's brows drew together fiercely as she rounded on Nell. 'Sorry? No, you're not.'

'We always knew Venice wasn't forever—'

'I'm not talking about Venice!'

'What, then?'

But Molly had already turned away. Anyway, Nell knew very well what she meant. She had tried to protect her, but you couldn't protect your child from life however hard you tried. Luca had come into their lives and now he was gone again, and Molly was grieving for him.

'Molly, please. Can't we talk about this?'

Molly snatched her arm away as Nell went to comfort her and kept staring fixedly out of the window. Nell didn't have to see her face to know that she was crying.

CHAPTER FOURTEEN

THE house was a flatter, duller place. Even his nephews and nieces were subdued for once, and his mother was hardly speaking to him.

No, that was wrong: she had managed one tirade over breakfast. He was a hard, unfeeling brute, apparently, without an ounce of tenderness in him. His glib answer that she was probably right had stayed with him throughout the day, nagging at him like a toothache. Was it his fault Nell had left Venice without warning, taking Molly with her? Did he suggest she leave his mother a note at some unearthly hour to say that she was leaving, the same note that had been flung at him across the breakfast table?

He had done the right thing. No man could live with the ghost of another man standing at his shoulder.

The house seemed cold when she opened it up, cold and unwelcoming. Molly went straight to her room and Nell heard her throw herself onto the bed.

'I'll go up, shall I?' Marianna suggested.

'No, leave her for a while. She'll have a sleep, and then she'll get over it.'

Nell pretended not to see Marianna's raised brow. She had

to protect Molly, but she couldn't have her dictating which path she should take through life. She had enough trouble getting that one right without outside interference.

'I'm going to make a coffee.' She smiled hopefully at Marianna. 'Would you like one?'

'No, you go right ahead. Coffee always keeps me awake, and I think Molly's got the right idea.'

Maybe Marianna was right, but there was no way she could follow her example, Nell realised as she walked into the kitchen.

And since when had the kitchen been so big, so empty, and the house so lonely?

Luca arrived home after the most strenuous workout at the gym he could remember. It was then he had one of the stranger telephone conversations of his life.

It concerned an unfinished game of Doom Merchant Seven, a little-known computer game, familiar only to aficionados of highly competitive techno-sport.

'So, you chickened out?'

Molly's voice was cold and hostile, and for a moment he couldn't work out what she was talking about.

'Molly?'

'Oh, so you do remember who I am?'

'Of course I remember.' He thought quickly, glancing at his watch. It was eleven o'clock at night. 'You got home safely?' He was playing for time, trying to think how best to handle the situation from his slim set of resources marked *fledgling personal relationships: care of.*

'Don't be silly. I wouldn't be talking to you if we hadn't.'

'How's your mother?' It was out before he could check himself.

'As if you care.'

That hurt.

'So…' Molly picked up where she had left off. 'You let me beat you that time, didn't you?'

She'd guessed. He got the picture now. Luca smiled wryly. Molly was smart.

'And now you're too chicken to play me for real, finish that game we started.'

'No—it's not that.'

'What, then?'

'You're in London, I'm in Venice.'

'And whose fault is that?'

He wasn't about to answer that one.

'I thought you cared about us…'

There was a long, ragged silence, during which he was sure he could hear Molly trying to stifle tears. The hard front, the cover story that had given her an excuse to call him, everything had dissolved into the shattered hopes of one small child. And he was just as guilty as Nell…thinking they could hide the way they felt about each other, when every glance, every accidental touch, even the charge in the air when they were in the same room gave the game away.

And he did care for Molly, more than she realised, more than he knew how to handle.

There was a loud sniff.

'So are you going to finish that game or not?'

He smiled, hearing the steel had returned to Molly's voice. It was the same steel her mother had.

They shouldn't have to be so brave. And he didn't have to be such a coward. What was really at risk here—his pride?

'Well?' Molly demanded.

He could picture the small face, pale brows drawn together, eyes fierce, lips firm, as Molly waited for his answer.

'I don't suppose you're going to let me off?'

'You got that right.'

* * *

'It's nice of you to go to so much trouble, Molly.'

Nice? It was a miracle, Nell thought, feeling a rush of relief as she surveyed the dining-room table. Molly had been surly and unresponsive on the flight home and had slept in until lunchtime the following day. The rest of Saturday had been spent in what Nell could only describe as a state of tension. She had waited for an explosion, which strangely didn't come. By Sunday morning the atmosphere in the house had reached crisis point, and the very last thing she had been expecting was that Molly would take it upon herself to lay the lunch table, cutting fresh flowers from the garden for a centrepiece and even rummaging in the dresser drawers to find the candles that only ever came out at Christmas. She took it as a sign that they were over the worst. Molly had decided to be brave about her break with Venice—and if Molly was happy then Nell was happy. She would just have to find a way to live with the ache in her heart.

Nell took particular care with the meal, and was just going to freshen up when she heard muffled giggles and bustling around in the hallway. 'Molly, who's there?' Thinking someone had arrived, she quickly tugged off her apron and blew the hair out of her eyes. Checking the roast wouldn't burn, she opened the kitchen door to find it wasn't someone arriving. It was two people leaving.

'Molly? Marianna? Where are you going? Lunch is almost ready.'

'Wish we could stay, Mum. Places to go…'

Nell's heart began to race. 'Oh, no. You wouldn't.' Her face froze. 'You have!'

Molly was avoiding her gaze, and Marianna had adopted her 'I haven't a clue what's going on' expression.

'Marianna, tell me what's happening. Molly!' Nell's voice

sharpened as Molly hurriedly opened the front door. 'I insist you tell me what you've done! It isn't funny—'

'Please don't be angry with her.'

They all looked up at the same time to see Luca, tall and tanned and immaculately dressed as ever, sheltering beneath the protective cover of Nell's storm porch with the rain sheeting down behind him.

Nell recovered first. Drawing on every reserve of strength she had, she said, 'Luca—what are you doing here?'

'I felt sure I would receive a warm welcome.' He slanted an ironic smile at her, and then turned to Molly. 'I brought you something.'

Molly had been hanging back, unsure of her mother's reaction to what might turn out to be the biggest mistake of her life. 'Really?' she said hesitantly.

Luca exchanged a brief glance with Nell to check he wasn't barred from bringing presents. At her small nod, he smiled. 'Doom Merchant Eight.'

'*Wicked!*'

'Leave her,' he murmured to Nell when Molly seized the package with indecent haste. 'Give me an hour with your mother, Molly, and then it's game on.'

'This time,' Nell interrupted, barring Molly and Marianna's path to the door, 'why don't we all eat together, and then you can go out with Marianna later, Molly?'

'I think we should give you some space, Mum.'

Nell wasn't sure she wanted to think too deeply about all the things she could see in Molly's eyes. 'All right, then. One hour.' She moved away from the door. 'I'll keep dinner warm for you.'

'Why did you walk out like that?' Luca asked. They were sitting in the kitchen nursing mugs of coffee while his jacket dried out.

'I thought it was best. For me, for Molly.'

'You could have said goodbye, Nell.'

'I didn't want to…'

'You didn't want to what?' he pressed when she fell silent.

'I didn't want to go over the past. I didn't want to dredge it all up again. I didn't know what I could say to convince you that I don't love Jake.'

Luca dipped his head in acknowledgement.

'You have no idea…' Her voice broke, and she had to wait a minute until she felt steady enough to speak. 'You can't imagine what was happening in my head when I walked into that hospital room…prepared for the worst, yes, but prepared to say goodbye to the man I loved, the man I thought loved me, the man I thought I could trust. My whole world stopped turning on that day. Everything I had believed in was a lie. Every decision I made, every thought I had was influenced by the fact that I wasn't one person, I was half of a couple. Now suddenly all that was snatched away. I didn't know who I was any more, and it took a long time to recover a sense of self-worth. It was only when Molly was born that I felt I had something to live for again.'

'It's not enough for anyone to be half of a couple,' Luca observed softly. 'But there's no reason why you can't be half of a couple and an individual as well. You have to retain your own identity. If half of a couple always leans and the other always props, that's not a real partnership.' He made a steeple with his fingers. 'Sometimes we all have to lean, and that's when you need to know there's someone there for you.'

'Unfortunately,' Nell's gaze brightened as she stared at him, 'I didn't have anyone to lean on. So I built a wall around myself.'

'And when Molly was born you took her into the stockade.'

'Until Marianna came along and injected some normality into our lives.'

'Marianna helped you as much as Molly, I think.'

'Oh, yes, she did. But…'

'There were certain things Marianna couldn't help you with?' Luca prompted wryly.

'I couldn't tell her that I felt—I felt a failure as a woman.'

Taking her hands, Luca drew them away from her face. 'Will you stop that? You're not a failure. You're a wonderful woman. Beautiful, desirable, kind…a wonderful mother, and a caring human being, which is perhaps the most important quality of all. Your husband was weak, and sometimes weak people can do more damage than we know.'

'I don't love him,' she said quietly.

'I know that. I'm sorry. Sometimes things seem to get so heated between us…so many frustrated hopes, desires, they erupt in a great storm like the lava in a volcano that can't be contained any longer. I know you're not that weak.'

She sighed. 'All I feel is pity for him now, because he lost his life, and regret because he ruined so many other lives.'

'He was just a coward. And he can't ruin your life unless you let him.'

'It's me that's the coward. I should never have run away from you.'

'You're not a coward. You're the most courageous woman I know. Look at how much good you've done in Venice. And bringing Molly up, making a life for yourself—how can you call yourself a coward?'

'I couldn't face you…'

'But everyone has a secret fear they'd rather not confront. For you that means risking your heart again. And this time you've got Molly to consider. Don't you think I understand that? Don't you know that's why I'm here? To make you believe you can trust me?'

As he drew her hands into his and held them tight, Nell began to smile. 'So you're not here because you've heard about my roast beef and Yorkshire pudding?'

'English food?' Luca flashed her an ironic smile, relieved to see her eyes were clear and bright. Cocking his head to one side, he observed wryly, 'It's safe to assume it wasn't the cooking that brought me here.'

'That was delicious, Nell.' Luca put down his napkin. 'You have changed my mind completely about English food in a single meal.'

'That's very kind of you.' Nell smiled. They had just finished eating and for once she hadn't burnt the carrots. 'But something tells me you didn't come all this way to talk about my cooking.'

'No. I wanted to talk to you, about you. About us.'

'Us?'

'Don't look so worried,' he said with a smile.

'Everything hinges on trust, doesn't it?'

'Yes, it does,' he agreed. 'But you can't expect trust to spring fully formed into a relationship. It takes time to build, to take root and twine around the person you care about. It's what binds you together, makes you feel safe, warm, confident.'

'You're an expert now?' Nell said wryly.

'No, and I don't pretend to be. I have trust issues too. I've had to learn to trust feelings, to interpret them as accurately as I interpret scientific information. I use gut instinct in my work as an adjunct to everything I learn from scientific testing, but I have a problem trusting that same instinct when it comes to human relationships. I didn't want to risk it either, Nell.'

'But you're learning?' Her eyes teased him.

'I hope you think so.' He was perfectly serious. 'And to prove it to you, I'd like you to read this.' Reaching into his breast pocket, Luca brought out a leaflet.

'What is it?' Nell held back.

'Take a look. Tell me what you think. I'm going to have it updated every year.'

Nell started to read out loud, "'Guidelines for visitors to Venice. What to expect if you are taken to hospital… Twenty-four-hour emergency numbers… Danger signs for parents to be aware of…'" Her voice tailed away. 'Why haven't you shown me this before?'

He shrugged. 'Because part of me wouldn't accept that I had learned so much from you when we first met. A terrible thing, pride.'

Nell started reading again. 'But this is good.'

'It was long overdue. You were right. I had a lot to learn in those days, and I hope this proves that I have tried to make changes. Your scheme is good, Nell. I'm going to keep it. Not because of the way I feel about you, but because I believe it is an improvement to the services we already offer—'

'Just a minute.' Laying her hand on Luca's sleeve, Nell stopped him. 'Can we just rewind for a moment?' When he frowned in bemusement she added in her business voice, 'I believe you said something about the way you feel about me?'

'Oh, that,' Luca murmured wryly, and his eyes were dancing with laughter.

The telephone interrupted their kiss, which was everything a kiss should be, Nell thought as she floated across the room.

'The cinema?' she said into the receiver. Her gaze flicked to Luca. 'But what about your computer game, Molly? And you haven't eaten yet… You have? You were starving…yes, I see.' She cut the connection, shaking her head. 'I hope you don't mind,' she said, turning to Luca, 'but you may have to wait a little longer for your contest.'

'I'll get over it,' Luca assured her, holding out his arms. 'Come here. How I've missed you.'

'I've only been gone a couple of days,' Nell pointed out as he drew her close.

'Exactly.'

When at last he let her go, he shot a glance through the window. 'Shall we go out?'

'Out?'

'For a walk.'

'But it's raining!'

'An adventure?' he suggested.

'Like a carnival in the rain?'

'Call it your one new and exciting challenge for today.'

'I prefer rain to eel, that's for sure.' She began to laugh.

'Marianna has a key, doesn't she?'

'Of course.'

'And you have a raincoat?'

'Hey, I live in England.'

'Then let's go out. I need to talk to you.'

They walked for miles. Nell was glad Luca had come prepared in a heavy waterproof jacket and sturdy shoes. The wet-weather look suited him, she mused as they walked along the pavement overlooking the river, arms entwined.

'Are you wet enough yet?' she teased when they stopped on top of a bridge from where they could look out over London. Water was dripping off their noses, and Luca's hair was hanging in his eyes. Even then he looked like the most temptation she'd seen since...since she'd last seen him, Nell thought, wondering how hard it would be to live without him.

Flicking the wet hair out of his eyes, Luca held her gaze. 'Would you consider exchanging all this for life in a crumbling *palazzo*?'

'What do you mean?'

'The rain,' he prompted. 'It would be quite a wrench leaving it, I imagine.'

'Oh, and Venice never floods?'

'At least we provide platforms so that people don't have to get their feet wet.'   —

'But you're not frightened to put your toe in the water, are you, Luca?'

He gave her a look of rebuke for the irony. 'I'm not frightened of anything.'

'You're such a man!'

'That's certainly true,' he agreed. 'Or at least it was the last time I looked. But you haven't answered my question yet, and I'm not going to let you run away from me this time.'

'Can you repeat the question?'

Putting his arms around her waist, Luca drew her close so their lips were almost touching. 'I have to say, this isn't exactly the way I had this planned in my mind.'

'So, you've been rehearsing what you're going to say to me. I can't wait. It must be good.'

'I hope you think so.'

'You only hope?' Nell teased.

'All right, I'm confident.' Luca grew serious. 'I'm saying I love you, Nell. I'm saying I can't live without you.' He exhaled with something like exasperation. 'Can't you see? The hospital misses you, my mother misses you, Paolo misses you—'

'Maria and Tomas miss me?'

'You have no idea.'

'But do you miss me?' Nell whispered, searching his eyes.

'More than you'll ever know. I need you. I love you so much, Nell. I want all of us to live together in Venice…'

'In Venice?'

'So you can help me to bring the old *palazzo* back to life.'

Nell couldn't control her smile. 'And you have another free labourer on hand?'

'Did you think I'd invite a weakling to share my life?'

She smiled. 'But—Molly…'

Touching a finger to her lips, Luca reassured her. 'I know you come as a package, Nell. That's one of your attractions.'

'Ah, now I understand. You get a games partner *and* a labourer.'

'I know a bargain when I see it.' Luca's smile faded but the warmth in his eyes grew. 'Will you marry me, Nell? I can't live without you,' he said simply. 'I love you more than life itself.'

'My answer's yes. And I love you too, Luca. More than you'll ever know.'

And they sealed their pledge with a very wet kiss.

HARLEQUIN®

Mediterranean NIGHTS™

Tycoon Elias Stamos is launching his newest luxury cruise ship from his home port in Greece. But someone from his past is eager to expose old secrets and to see the Stamos empire crumble.

Mediterranean Nights
launches in June 2007 with...

FROM RUSSIA, WITH LOVE
by *Ingrid Weaver*

Join the guests and crew of *Alexandra's Dream* as they are drawn into a world of glamour, romance and intrigue in this new 12-book series.

HARLEQUIN *Presents*

Mediterranean Brides

**Two billionaires, one Greek, one Spanish—
will they claim their unwilling brides?**

Meet Sandor and Miguel, men who've taken all the prizes
when it comes to looks, power, wealth and arrogance.
Now they want marriage with two beautiful women.
But this time, for the first time, both Mediterranean
billionaires have met their matches and it will take more
than money or cool to tame their unwilling mistresses—
try seduction, passion and possession!

Eleanor Wentworth has always been unloved and
unwanted. Greek tycoon Sandor Christofides has wealth
and acclaim—all he needs is Eleanor as his bride.
But is Ellie just a pawn in the billionaire's game?

BOUGHT:
THE GREEK'S BRIDE
by Lucy Monroe

On sale June 2007.